TIGHTROPE

Harem of Freaks Book 5

CRYSTAL ASH

MELODY

Outwardly I smiled, but my insides twisted upon themselves. I kept glancing toward the trees where Hunter and his pups had run off to.

His pack was here, his family and loved ones from before he got captured, before he ever met me and Connor. I should have been happy, like everyone else was. While Hunter froze in shock at hearing his brothers' howls, Raz lifted him from the chair and booted him toward the woods, much to Connor and Arjun's amusement.

The pups were so happy, yelping and howling as they took off toward the woods. Everyone expressed excitement and happiness at Hunter being united with his family. He deserved it after being separated from them and losing his mate.

So why couldn't I fight this dread settling over me?

Only Arjun seemed to notice something off with me, his blue-green eyes nearly glowing in the fading light.

"Penny for your thoughts?" the cheeky tiger shifter asked me.

He leaned back in his seat lazily, one arm up and resting behind his head, the other draped over his belly. All seven of us, kids included, just polished off a massive pot of curry he made. Our bellies were full, but his was still as taut and flat as ever. Come to think of it, all the guys still had their washboard stomachs, and I was the only one carrying a food baby.

And possibly a real baby.

Shit, don't think about that.

But that also weighed on my mind and might've been partially responsible for this feeling of dread. I needed to tell Connor and soon, but I wasn't about to spill all that to Arjun, even if he was attempting to not be a dick.

"I just wonder if they'll force him to choose," I voiced aloud. "Between them or us. They probably hate humans and he always made it seem like wolf packs are really strict."

And not all families were good. I got a harsh reminder of that when we visited my old home before coming into Georgia. My heart ached for my younger siblings, who had no choice but to put up with my raging alcoholic monster of a mother. I needed to get them out. We had the space now in this amazing house, but it would still be complicated to do legally.

"They can't force him to do anything," Raz said with a soft growl, leveling his steel-gray eyes at me. "He's a strong wolf. Have some faith in him, *steluța*. He'll only do what he feels is best."

"You're right," I told him with a smile. "I know you're right, dragon."

Minutes crawled, and no wolves emerged from the forest. The sun finally set, and the mosquitos came out in full force, so we packed up the dishes and headed back inside. It was still too early to go to bed, but I'd be pacing back and forth in front of the window, waiting for my white wolf to return if I didn't do something.

Arjun, the apparent perceptive one of the night, seemed to sense my need for a distraction.

"Why don't you tell me about your shaman abilities?" he suggested with a light touch to my shoulder. "And we'll see what you can work on."

I looked at him, surprised. He was really on his best behavior tonight. First making curry to make up for jabbing at my upbringing, now this. After Raz and I rescued him from that awful carnival, we kept getting off on the wrong foot. Everyone chalked it up to him being English and me not getting his sense of humor. Maybe I was sensitive, but I couldn't help that it hurt he didn't seem to like me. Not even a thank you for saving his big striped, orange ass.

His accent didn't help, nor his eyes that looked like the bluish-green of a tropical ocean. For that matter, neither did his caramel skin, his inky black hair, or his tall, powerful build similar to Hunter's.

"You're being awfully helpful tonight," I remarked, my voice laced with skepticism.

He shrugged and stepped away from me, his hands raised. "It's just an offer. You're clearly distressed at no longer being attached to your wolf's hip, so thought I'd provide some entertainment until he comes back."

"I am *not* attached to his hip," I retorted, crossing my

arms. "He runs off into the woods all the time. I don't care if he's away from me for a while."

"It's a joke," Arjun sighed. "Learn to take one, for fuck's sake."

My shoulders sagged. He was right. I was being tense and uptight for no reason. Just that one time.

"Fine," I said. "Who knows when such an offer will come again?"

"It's a standing offer," he answered. "You're always welcome to come to me with questions." His mouth split into a grin. "Just a matter of whether or not you can tolerate my presence."

"The curry helped but you're on thin ice, buddy." I laughed awkwardly, pushing hair out of my face. Shit, was that really the best I could do?

"I'll behave," he grinned. "Tonight."

"That's all I can ask for. So how do we do this?"

"Let's go somewhere quiet." He nodded toward the far corner of the theater room, sectioned off by a half wall and rows of bookshelves.

"Where are you two going?" Connor lifted an eyebrow as he wheeled past us into the kitchen. I glared at him in reply. So nosy.

"Just stealing your girl out from under your nose, human," Arjun announced joyfully, throwing an arm over my shoulders.

"Not true!" I glared at the infuriatingly handsome tiger shifter, pulling away from under his arm. "Thin ice, remember?"

"Trust me, dove. I'm holding back a lot."

"We're practicing shaman stuff." I grumbled to Connor,

making a shooing motion with my hands. "Go, I can't be distracted."

"Mm-hmm," he mused skeptically, as he directed his wheelchair away. Raz grinned at me, leaning against a kitchen counter as Connor approached him.

I tuned out their low voices, chatting as Arjun and I made our way to the reading corner. He sat cross-legged on the floor and gestured for me to follow suit. I stayed well out of touching range, which he didn't object to.

"So why don't you give me a rundown of what you've experienced?" he began, resting his elbows on his knees.

"It started with dreams pretty quickly after I met Hunter and the pups for the first time," I began. "I saw from the perspectives of other shifters. That's how I learned about you. Then I started feeling their animal instincts and abilities. Apparently I could take on their forms and give off their... presence or what have you."

"Like when Connor sensed an animal in bed next to him once," he said knowingly.

"Yes," I blinked, surprised. I didn't know they had been talking to Arjun about this stuff. "Before we rescued you, Raz said my eyes changed color. I grew long teeth and sprouted fur on my face. That was when I was trying to talk to you, the human, but only your tiger was responding to me and I felt... your tiger's instincts."

I didn't want to say I felt his bloodthirst, the desire to kill, and his power to do it. After seeing him kill the ringmaster from his own perspective, it still churned my stomach.

"When did you start communicating with your mind?" he asked, his blue-green gaze curious and focused on me.

"Back in Crying Falls," I replied. "I rode on Raz in

dragon form, and just directed a thought to him and he answered. It was crazy."

"Very interesting," he mused, stroking the dark stubble that began to appear on his jaw. "A shaman's abilities are usually separated and very distinct from each other. Yours seem to have them all blended together."

"What do you mean?"

"When my stepfather trained his apprentice, he focused on only Sight for the first year," he explained. "That's the ability to see through a shifter's eyes. The next year was Sense, being able to feel the instincts and desires of the animal you're focusing on. And it took a whole three years to master Semblance, the ability to throw the illusion that you are an animal as well."

"What about the mind communication? Telepathy, or whatever."

"It's called Speak," Arjun said softly. "Not every shaman has it. In fact, it's incredibly rare."

"Seriously?"

He nodded slowly. "My stepfather's grandmother was the last known shaman to Speak."

"That's... crazy." I rocked back, placing my hands behind me on the floor. "I might not have been able to save you in time if I couldn't talk to you."

"You are correct." He mimicked my posture, leaning back with his hands behind him. "Quite serendipitous, isn't it?"

"Seems that way," I admitted. "Like I was supposed to find you to figure all this shit out."

"The universe has a funny way of unfolding on us," he grinned.

HUNTER

I ran in the direction of those howls, my heart crashing against my ribs. Even in wolf form, my human emotions bled over. I felt the tension in my stomach, the all too human hope of seeing my brothers again daring to rise.

Colt, Gabe. Can it really be you guys?

I had to prepare to be wrong. The disappointment would be too great if I dared to hope too much.

My paws carried me soundlessly to a boulder, where I paused and let out a warning howl. The pups, who had raced off ahead of me, came back to wait under my rock. Roo whined. Rinna's tail wagged rapidly. They missed their family too and were dying to see them. But they had to stay by me.

I growled a warning at them to emphasize staying near me before I jumped off, loping at a slower pace toward the howls.

With a quick sniff in the air, my pulse went into overdrive. Yes, those were their scents. The scents I picked up temporarily while out in these woods the other day. They had been so faint then, I thought it was an old trail. But now the scent was fresh, bringing back powerful memories of playing together as pups and running proudly with our pack.

I followed the trail carefully, my nose to the ground to pick up any possible scents of danger. Roo and Rinna whined and pawed at me, running in circles and through my legs. They were eager to see their uncles, but I would not take any chances of endangering them again.

We reached the stream where we drank and rested the other day, and across the water, I saw two canine silhouettes that looked remarkably like mine. Their smell was overpowering, the scent of family, warmth, and familiarity. I wanted to run over and hug them, but I stood my ground and let out a warning growl.

Their shapes, dark and shadowy in the fading light, shifted and stretched tall as they took on their human forms.

"Can you believe it, Gabe?" one of them said. "He doesn't even recognize us, but the pups do."

"Uncle Colt!" Rinna squealed. The pups shifted too and practically vibrated with excitement.

God damn it.

I shifted to human myself, already splashing across the stream before I even had fully formed human feet.

"You goddamn sons of bitches," I choked out, clapping my arms around Colt in a rough bear hug before turning to Gabe and doing the same.

"Glad to see you too, bro," Gabe laughed, slapping my back. "Thought I was going nuts when I picked up your scent out here."

"Christ almighty, look at you." Colt grabbed the back of my neck, ruffling my hair with his other hand. As my oldest brother, he often took a fatherly role with me and now was no different.

He examined my face, affectionately slapping my cheek with a wide grin. "You look good, little ghost. I'd even venture to say you look happy."

"A lot has happened," I said, my own grin threatening to split my face. "Jesus, I never thought I'd see you two again!"

"Uncle Colt!" Roo shouted from the ground, practically wrapping himself around Colt's leg like he did with Mel.

"Ah, I've missed you, little man." Colt picked him up and settled him against his side. "Have you been taking care of your dad?"

"Yes, sir!" Roo bobbed his head emphatically. "And Miss Mel, too!"

"Oh really, who's that?" Colt cast a questioning glance at me while Gabe picked up a squirming, giggling Rinna and proceeded to tickle her.

"She's a human," I said quickly, before Roo could blurt out anything else. "And a shaman. She rescued us from the carnival and we've been with her ever since."

"A shaman?" Colt's eyes narrowed.

"Been with her?" Gabe asked at the same time, turning Rinna upside down. "What do you mean?"

"Traveling with her," I said lamely, although with one look I knew they could see through it. "She's a carnival ringmistress. After she freed us, I stuck around and filled in a spot in a carnival for her."

"You *what?*" Colt growled, disdain in his eyes.

"I volunteered. She didn't want me to," I replied,

holding his gaze. "But she saved all of us, so I felt like I owed her. She's a good person, amazing even. And I—" my voice choked, and I swallowed. "I didn't have anyone else. I couldn't pick up any of your scents and thought I lost you all for good."

"Sounds like you're in love with her," Gabe observed. "A *human*."

"A shaman," Colt repeated, folding his arms under Roo's legs. "That certainly makes things interesting."

"You know about them?" I asked.

"Not much." He looked over at Gabe. "We met our first one recently."

Gabe snorted, setting Rinna down on the ground. "And what a fuckin' brat she is."

My eyes shifted between my two brothers. Clearly, they had some disagreements about this subject.

Colt chuckled a bit patronizingly. Gabe was younger than me, and Colt often made sure he knew it.

"I for one think they can be useful," Colt said. "Miriam's saved our asses a few times."

"Our instincts would have done the same," Gabe retorted snappily. "I say let's keep it simple and not trust any humans. Then we'll never run the risk of getting hunted or sold to carnivals! How easy is that?"

"It's not that simple," Colt replied. "You're still a human yourself, runt. A true wolf pack would have left you for dead, but thanks to our humanity, you're still around to be a pain in my ass."

"I'm no runt," Gabe snarled.

"You overcompensate like one," Colt muttered.

"Guys, guys." I stepped between them to interrupt their growling and teeth gnashing. "This is supposed to be a happy reunion, right? It feels like years since I've seen you both."

"The middle child is right," Colt laughed. "Enough talk of shamans for now, let's hunt! Let's bring down a kill and feast like we used to." He looked between Roo and Rinna, bouncing Roo on his side like he used to when my boy was an infant. "What do you guys say? Want to hunt with your dad and your old uncles?"

"Yeah!" the pups cried in unison, already shifting as Colt set Roo down.

My older brother looked at me while the pups yipped excitedly around our ankles.

"We've got a lot to talk about," he said solemnly. "About you, us, and the state of the pack right now, but all that can wait." Colt's jaws elongated, his teeth already snapping with the anticipation of a kill. Before losing his ability to speak, he added, "Right now, let's just celebrate being alive."

MELODY

With my head resting on Connor's brawny chest, and the heat of Razvan's skin pressed against my back, I couldn't feel any more comfortable, safe, and secure.

But sleep wouldn't come. My eyes stayed glued to the moon out the window in the dark sky. I kept the window cracked so I could listen to any howls. The clock read 1:22 am, but I was wide awake. And I knew I'd remain awake until Hunter came back.

I thought about using Speak or Sight to get a sense of what he was doing, just to check that he was okay, but I resisted. I would know if something bad happened to him. He deserved private time with his family.

But we're *his family,* a stubborn voice in my head reminded me.

Raz groaned in his sleep behind me, shifted his position, and wrapped an inked arm tighter around my waist. His cheek brushed against my back like a soft, sweeping kiss.

You have to come back, Hunter, I thought, lacing my fingers with Raz's at my belly. *For both of us.*

He shifted again behind me and rubbed his thumb across my palm.

"Still awake, *steluța?*" he asked groggily.

"Just can't sleep," I whispered. "Don't worry about me. I'll fall asleep, eventually."

"You saying that is automatically going to make me worry about you," he chuckled, gently pulling me away from Connor so he wrapped around me even tighter with my head resting on his bicep. "What's on your mind?"

"I'll give you three guesses."

"Hunter, Roo, Rinna," he murmured, nuzzling at me sleepily.

"Congratulations, you win a prize."

"Heh, I already have my prize." He ran a hand over my hip and down the length of my thigh. "Are you afraid he's going to leave us?"

"I don't know. Maybe subconsciously?" I wondered. "Rationally, I don't think he would. But aside from you guys, every man in my life has left me at some point."

He said nothing for a few moments, just tenderly ran his hands over my skin. Honestly, that was enough. He listened, and he was there.

"I wish I could tell you that won't happen," he whispered. "But I've been proven wrong about people many times. I've had friends who let me down badly. I've had people who barely knew me accept me like one of their own." He squeezed me for a brief moment. "Like you."

"And you're stuck with me," I teased, looking at him over my shoulder. "I'm not letting you go no matter what."

"There's no one else I'd rather be stuck with," he

replied. "If it came down to choosing, I want you to know that I would always choose you over Hunter."

I flipped around to face him, my fingers tracing the contours of his neck and jaws in the darkness.

"I'd never make you choose. You know that, right? You're all so amazing to me, I could never choose in a million years. How could I ask you to do what I can't?"

"Just in the event that Hunter forces a decision," he explained. "Or whatever other unforeseen circumstance happens."

My fingers found his lips, and then my mouth did. He kissed me hard as he pulled me tight against him, bringing my leg over his hip.

"Can you stay quiet?" he whispered, his split tongue caressing the side of my neck.

"What—ah..."

His hand secure on my ass, he rolled his hips against me. The motion was slow, almost lazy, but his flesh was hot and growing harder as he pressed against me. I clung to his shoulders, matching his movement as his heat lit me ablaze.

"Don't want to wake up sleeping beauty over there," he chuckled, pressing against my slickening core as his cock grew stiff and thick with every breath.

Behind me, Connor slept like the dead, snoring softly.

"He's going to be pissed he didn't get to join in," I giggled.

"I don't care," Raz whispered with a soft growl. "As hot as it is to share you, I like having you to myself."

With that, he pressed inside me, and I bit my lip to hold in the moan. I lifted my leg higher on his side and he muffled his own moan into the pillow as he surged into me deeper.

"Bite me when you want to scream," he rasped. "I want to feel how good I'm making you feel."

My teeth immediately found the taut skin of his shoulder, the hard muscle moving under my mouth as he thrust into me.

When my first orgasm came, turning me into a hot, shuddering mess from his effortless thrusts, I wondered if I ruined one of his tattoos from biting him so hard. My teeth still clamped down on him, he rolled me over on my back and fucked me with same slow, rolling thrusts.

He moaned so hotly into my neck and the pillow under my head. Seemed I wasn't the only one having a hard time keeping quiet. I could feel how much he was holding back from the tension in his body. He wanted to fuck me until the headboard slammed against the wall and made Connor literally fall out of bed.

But I liked this quietness too. It was naughty and intimate. I loved hearing the variance in his breathing, feeling his restraint, and letting him know my pleasure in ways other than noise. He hummed as my nails dug into his back. My teeth in his shoulder made him curse under his breath and deepen his thrusts. He kissed my neck so deliciously every time my head fell back with a gasp.

I came one more time when his cock turned to iron inside me, right before his own release with a shuddering growl. Then only the sound of our heavy, panting breaths filled the room.

"That was more difficult than I thought it would be," he laughed under his breath as he slid out of me, pulling me against his chest where his heart hammered like a drum.

"Hotter than I thought it would be," I said, curling up against his side.

"Mm, and I have the marks to prove it," he agreed, his fingers drifted over my hair. "Think you'll be relaxed enough to sleep now?"

"Oh, was that your plan all along?" I teased, circling a finger around one of his nipples.

"Maybe." He grabbed my hand. "Stop, that tickles."

"You seduced me with your ulterior motives!" I laughed quietly, reaching for his other nipple with my free hand. He caught that one too, and soon we were wrestling playfully as he tried to keep my hands away. Connor only groaned once and flopped onto his side, facing away from us. I swore that man could sleep through a hurricane.

Unsurprisingly, I stood no chance against Raz, and he had me pinned within a minute. He somehow crossed my arms over my chest, then held them down with his arms as he settled back into cuddling, holding me against him and sighing happily.

"Hey," I whispered, wriggling against my bonds. "Let me turn around. I want to tell you something."

"Hm, I don't know about that," he said with a playful kiss on my neck. "You've got tricks, woman."

"I'm serious, Raz."

He loosened his hold enough to let me spin in his arms to face him again. My hands rested on his chest, where his heart began slowing down to normal. He caressed my hair out of my face as he waited for me to speak.

"What is it?" He tried not to sound concerned, but I knew he was.

"I love you, Raz," I whispered. "I have for a while. I'm sorry I wasn't able to say it earlier."

Underneath my hands, his heartbeat sped up like an animal breaking into a run. In the darkness, I still saw his smile break out, so beautiful and unrestrained.

"And I love you, *steluţa,*" he returned. "So utterly and completely. Don't be sorry. I don't ever want you to tell me something before you're ready."

Our mouths found each other again, pressing in a warm, sensual dance as we sank into this glow, this love we didn't have to hide anymore. I was so grateful to him for his patience and sweetness that lived beneath his hard, tattooed exterior. Even then, I still loved his roughness and the way he took my body without apology, without treating me like I might break.

He also successfully got my mind off of Hunter, which I appreciated.

My hands drifted in the midst of our kiss, caressing down his chest now that his guard was down.

And his nipples ripe for tickling.

"Ah! You little—!"

He batted my hands away and reached to pin me again. Laughing, I let him grab me and pull me against him. While he muttered curses about my sneakiness, I snuggled in his warmth, utterly content.

Sleep must have taken over me eventually because the next thing I knew, soft light filtered through the window and voices murmured in the kitchen downstairs. Some voices I didn't recognize.

I lifted my head to find Raz gone, but Connor still sleeping. He rested on his stomach, arms under his pillow. His sculpted shoulders and back rose and fell with his breath.

"Hey," I whispered, sliding over to him. "You're getting your first prototypes put on today." I kissed his neck and the top of his back until he stirred and groaned beneath me.

"Mmm. Mornin', babe."

Not a minute passed before the deep breathing resumed.

"You're always so slow to get up," I teased, swatting his perky ass before climbing out of bed to get dressed.

"Hmm?" he rolled onto his back to look at me with one sleepy eye. "Why would I get up when I have this amazing view from bed?"

"Stop." I rolled my eyes but hid my grin as I pulled my shirt over my head. Raz inside me during the night and Connor admiring me first thing in the morning? How did a girl like me get so lucky?

My Marine lifted his head from the pillow and squinted as if he was concentrating.

"Is Hunter back?"

"I don't know," I admitted, my stomach fluttering nervously. "Someone's here, though."

He sat up, pushed back the covers, and stretched. "Hand me my clothes, babe? I'm going down with you."

I grabbed him clean underwear, shorts, and a tee and handed them to him, taking note that he chose to ask me for help. On any other day, he'd get out of bed and walk on his hands to get to his clothing himself. But it was easier to ask me. My stubborn Marine was trying to not be so stubborn, bless him.

We headed for the stairs together. I recognized Hunter's voice immediately upon leaving the bedroom, along with two others I never heard before. His brothers, most likely.

I paused, reaching deep into the shaman side of me to gather more information. I sensed dense gray fur, long slender snouts filled with canine teeth. Silent paws and sensitive black noses. Yep, definitely wolf shifters.

Connor gave my leg an affectionate caress with his hand as he walked himself down the steps. A simple reminder he was there for me, no matter what.

I descended the stairs to find all the shifters in the kitchen, Raz, Arjun, and the pups included. Two men I'd never seen before stood next to Hunter. The older one had his same golden eyes and tall, slender build, but dark wavy hair that reached his shoulders. His hair had a few streaks of grey, like he was in his mid-thirties.

The younger one was shorter, but still not *short* by any means. His height matched Razvan's. I stopped at the bottom of the stairs because he gave me an unmistakably dirty look. His dark auburn hair was straighter, like Hunter's. If it weren't for his scowl pointed in my direction, he would've been handsome, with freckles dotting over pale skin and sharp green eyes.

"Ah, the two-legged specimens arise," Arjun announced. "Mornin' to you both."

"You're hilarious, RJ." Connor settled into his wheelchair and breezed into the kitchen, ignoring the two strangers and heading straight for the pot of coffee. He would be an insufferable grump until he got a couple of cups in him and didn't care who knew it.

"I didn't mean anything by it, mate," Arjun giggled. "Not my best though."

"Connor, Mel." Hunter cleared his throat awkwardly. "This is Colt," he gestured to the older man next to him, "and Gabe. My brothers."

"Nice to meet you both." I offered a smile despite Gabe's frown and Colt staring at Connor's legs like he was growing aliens from his stumps. Nothing better than killing with kindness, right?

Gabe merely grunted at me before turning away to play with the kids on the floor.

"Hey, man." Connor whipped around from the counter. "I'm only saying this once. I get that y'all aren't the biggest fans of humans, but you're in *my* house and Mel's the shaman who saved your brother's ass. The least you can do is be respectful. If you're not, I'm kicking y'all out."

An uncomfortable silence hung heavily over the kitchen. Even the kids stopped playing and froze. Raz and Arjun tried to hide their smiles behind their hands.

Finally, Colt let out a soft laugh as he thumped Hunter on the chest. "The human with no feet has the bite of an alpha. I like it."

"I'm waiting, dude." Connor ignored the compliment and remained staring pointedly at Gabe, whose eyes shifted toward Colt as if waiting for instruction.

"My apologies," Gabe said, returning his gaze to me. "It's nice to meet you, too."

"It's alright." My smile didn't waver. If there was one thing I was good at, it was smiling through awkward situations.

"We hunted last night," Hunter announced. "We brought down an excellent buck and have been skinning and preparing it all morning. The first cuts are in the smoker outside and they'll be ready soon."

"We helped!" Roo added proudly. "We hunted like a real wolf pack again!"

"We sure did, buddy. We got him like this!" Gabe picked him up and growled menacingly as he tickled and kissed his nephew, while the pup squealed with laughter.

Colt struck up a conversation with Connor while Gabe proceeded to tickle attack Rinna as well. With his brothers occupied, Hunter made a beeline straight toward me.

"Sorry about Gabe," he muttered, lowering his forehead to mine. "My brothers have run into another shaman who's helped them, but he's still resistant to having any involvement with humans."

"It's okay." My heart fluttered at the closeness of him, his strong, lean body towering over me. It felt like so long since I felt him and only him this close, it took a moment to register what he said. "Wait, another shaman?"

"Yeah, I could hardly believe it myself." He slid his arms around my waist. "Her name is Miriam."

"I'd like to meet her if possible."

"I'll ask Colt," he smiled. "He seems fond of her."

My fingers trailed up his arms, tracing the long, slender muscles. "I missed you last night. I wish you told me you were going to be gone the entire night."

His handsome face fell. "I'm sorry, I didn't plan on it. I didn't believe it was really them until I saw them with my own eyes. We hunted to celebrate coming back together."

"I understand." I smiled up at him. "I just didn't know when I'd see you again."

My wolf pulled me tight against him with a soft growl, the sides of my shirt clenched in his fists.

"I'll always come back to you," he whispered, his eyes burning into mine. "Always."

"It's not just me you have to come back to, you know." My eyes shifted over to Razvan, who talked quietly with Arjun.

He took my chin in his hand to return my gaze back to him. Those golden eyes looked at me with all the sharp brightness of two suns.

"No one replaces you for me," he insisted. "Not even him."

4

CONNOR

I wasn't sure how to feel about these new wolves. Part of me wanted to give them the benefit of the doubt because they were Hunter's brothers. Not to mention his kids just adored and idolized their uncles.

But the younger one just pissed me the hell off. Mel made an effort to be nice, and he was just a rude piece of shit. They wouldn't have a fancy-ass smoker for the deer they killed if it wasn't for her getting me to come here.

I guzzled down my coffee in the now too-crowded kitchen, then wheeled toward the front door, eager for some fucking peace and fresh air.

"Let's go, babe." I pulled the door open and propped it against my chair, waiting for her to finish up with Hunter.

He gave her a long, lingering kiss and whispered something, to which she smiled and gave a small nod before coming to join me. As he turned to watch her go, I looked at him and made sure he saw me. His smile faded, and he returned my serious expression. The pale wolf was a perceptive guy. He'd get the message.

Satisfied for the moment, I left with Mel to walk the path leading to the main building of the FDR Center for Disabled Veterans.

"What was that about?" she asked once we were a few yards from the house. "You joining the wolf pack in some staring contest for alpha or something?"

"Nah," I answered. "Just reminding our wolf boy what's important."

"And what's that?"

"His brothers are guests in our house. *My* house, which I only have thanks to you. Which Hunter and his kids live in comfortably, thanks to you. They have one chance to shit on our hospitality, and Gabe already blew it. One more act of disrespect to you or any of us and they're fucking gone. I don't even care if it makes the kids cry. And Hunter needs to know not to tolerate that shit. If he makes excuses for them treating you like shit, I'll kick him out too."

"Damn," she breathed as if in disbelief, but smiled down at me warmly. "I don't often see your Marine side come out anymore, but I guess he's still in there."

"My only mission now is eliminating threats to your happiness." I released one wheel to grab her hand as she walked alongside me. "Plus, I only had one cup of coffee so I'm still fuckin' grumpy."

"I knew that had something to do with it," she laughed, threading her fingers through mine. "And I love that my grumpy Marine still defends my honor so valiantly."

"You are never the cause of my grumpiness, babe." I brought her palm to my lips and kissed it. "It's every other limp-dicked piece of shit out there."

"Oh my god, Connor," she groaned, slapping her other hand to her forehead but couldn't prevent the smile from escaping. Nor the shake of her shoulders as she tried to hold in her giggle.

I chuckled, pleased with myself as our scenic walk neared its end and the stark white building loomed up in front of us. Little did she know that I said that ridiculous shit for her reactions. She rolled her eyes, groaned, and *Oh, Connor*'d me, but I knew she secretly found it hilarious.

We said good morning to the physical therapy staff as we entered the building. At this point, we'd gotten to know most of them pretty well. The male therapists' eyes lingered a little too long on Mel and they greeted her enthusiastically, while greeting me cordially at best.

I almost gave them a piece of my mind the first time —she was *not* a piece of meat and not up for sharing outside of who she chose, but it wasn't necessary. She always responded politely, while holding my hand like now or her arm around my shoulder. Last time, she even sat down on my lap as I wheeled us to my therapy session.

It filled me with pride that I didn't need to get all territorial and claim her. She claimed me all on her own.

This time, Dr. Selow himself waited for us in our usual spot.

"Connor! How are you this morning?" He clapped me on the shoulder with a broad grin, looking more excited than I was. "Ready to try on some legs?"

"Man, I've been waiting to hear those words all week," I told him.

It was true, but a nugget of fear nestled in the back of my brain. It had been ages since I used what little leg muscles I had. Would I even have the strength to walk upright on my own?

"Right on, man! I'll be right back. I wanted to do the honors myself."

He left the room, and I lifted myself out of the chair to the bench against the wall. It was higher off the ground and would allow enough room to adjust the legs on me if necessary.

I gripped the edge of the bench, swinging my stumps back and forth like an anxious kid at the doctor's office. My nerve pain that put me in the hospital had been completely nonexistent for several days. Aside from not being able to walk, I felt right as rain.

I was nervous about the pain coming back from the pressure of the prosthetics, but Dr. Selow assured me after multiple tests that it wouldn't. And anyway, I knew not to push myself again like last time. I scared the hell out of my girl, pushed her away, and almost succeeded in losing her. I wouldn't make that same mistake again.

Mel came up next to me, leaning against the bench, and placed a small kiss on my shoulder.

"What're you thinking about?"

"Honestly?" I replied, nuzzling my forehead against hers. "Fucking you in a standing position."

"Connor..."

Dr. Selow returned with another man in a white lab coat, each of them carrying something wrapped in gray cloth, and Mel jumped away from me as if we got caught. I smiled inwardly. *Babe, we haven't even gotten started yet.*

"Connor, Mel, this is Dr. Lawson, the prosthetist who designed these prototypes for you. He's going to see how they fit and take note of any discomfort you have to make adjustments on future designs. Sound good?"

"Great." I drummed on my thighs, more out of anxiety than anything else. "Let's do it."

Dr. Selow smirked and paused before lifting the cover off of the prosthetic he held. Dr. Lawson followed his lead like they were unveiling priceless antiques at an auction or some shit.

But the pieces they held made my jaw drop. Even Mel let out a soft gasp. Smooth and sleek carbon steel laid across their palms. I knew they were using the latest technology, but those things looked straight up from the future, like robot legs. In short, fucking sweet.

"Nice and light, for less stress on your hip and knee joints." Dr. Lawson gently tossed his leg, my right leg, up in the air a few inches and caught it again. "I also equalized the weight between them so even though they're different lengths, one won't feel heavier than the other."

"There are sensors here too that'll detect when certain muscles flex," Dr. Selow pointed inside where my thigh would fit, "which will make the toes and ankle portions flex and move as if it were a real foot. Your balance will feel a lot more natural this way."

"I'll be damned," I laughed lightly, unable to take my eyes off the sleek, beautiful limbs. "You got my hopes up so high now, I'm almost scared to put 'em on."

"Remember, these are just prototypes," Dr. Lawson reminded me. "They may not work perfectly right out of the box, but we'll tweak and adjust whatever we need to."

"Put 'em on, babe." Mel squeezed my arm excitedly, shooting me a smile that made my heart flip-flop in my chest. My woman, my love. The one who never stopped believing in me. I couldn't be happier that she was at my side for this.

"Alright, Docs," I waved my arm, gesturing them forward. "Let's see how they fit."

Only ten minutes later, after a bit of adjusting and securing, I looked down at my robotic feet. With Mel's hand still on my bicep, I pushed off the bench and stood up.

I turned around in a small circle and looked at her.

"Hey," she grinned up at me, standing on tiptoes. "You're taller than before."

"The longer limbs assist with better range of motion," Dr. Lawson explained.

"Walk around a bit, Connor," Dr. Selow suggested, beaming.

I held my arms out at my side as I took more steps around the room. My balance was already excellent from my stilt-walking, but I'd still have to get used to these. I felt almost too teetering, like on the verge of losing my balance but not quite. Mainly, I was distracted by all the sensations. I could feel the ground beneath my feet, only I felt it in my thigh muscles. It didn't entirely make sense to me, but then again, I wasn't a fucking prosthetic limb engineer.

"Try balancing on one foot, then roll your ankle around on the other foot," Dr. Selow suggested.

I did as he said, realizing that I could sense how much weight I was putting into one leg. My foot rotated around as if it was actually connected to my body.

"How is it doing that?" I said in an awed whisper.

"Your brain is still connected to the leg muscle you have here," Dr. Selow pointed to my quad. "The prosthetic legs' sensors are so sensitive, they identify the muscle fibers you use for certain movements and when they're activated, the computer chip inside then tells the leg to do that motion, as fast as if it were coming from your brain."

"Amazing," Mel whispered. "It's like magic."

"Almost," Dr. Lawson chuckled. "It's science."

I walked a few more laps around the room, practicing squats, kicks, and other motions the doctors suggested.

"Any pain, Connor?" Dr. Selow asked. "Or discomfort?"

"None at all," I said, bouncing on the balls of my new feet. "Balance was a little off at first, but I'm getting the hang of it now. Feels great, actually."

"Excellent," Dr. Lawson grinned. "You're welcome to take this set home today and see how it feels after a few hours of wear. You still don't want to overdo it. Use the chair as your primary means of moving and gradually work up to these over time."

"Sure," I said dismissively, doing a few high-knee jumps. *I wonder if I can do a back flip in these...*

"Connor," Mel said in that adorable stern voice with an equally adorable stern look.

"I know, babe." I leaned over to plant a kiss on those pouty lips. "I'll listen to the doctors. God knows you'll give me hell if I don't."

"Smart woman," Dr. Selow chuckled. "Alright, you're welcome to exercise here or head home to try them out. Call us if anything's off with them."

"Thank you, doctors," Mel and I said together as they left the room.

"What's that naughty look for?" she demanded as soon as we were alone.

"What?" My smirk widened into a grin. "I just want to try something."

"Connor, what—"

I stuck one leg out and vaulted it over my head, the other one following. The world spun in a quick circle, and then my feet touched down less than a second later. A thrill I hadn't felt in ages surged within me.

"Backflips already?" Mel crossed her arms, but her eyes shone with pride.

"I landed it, didn't I?" I crossed the room to her and pulled those sexy hips against mine. She let out a little gasp, which I silenced with a kiss.

Damn, it felt so fucking good to kiss her like this. Her body flush against mine, standing on tiptoes to reach my mouth. I knew she didn't care about me having legs or not, but I felt like a man again holding her like this. Finally, I could dominate my woman again in the way I craved.

She let out a soft moan as my tongue pried her lips apart, her soft body molding to my hard torso as I pressed her against the wall. I broke the kiss only to lower myself and grab under her thighs, lifting her legs off the ground to wrap around my waist.

"Connor," she said in a breathy whisper, her face flushed. "Here?"

"I told you I wanted to conduct these very important tests as soon as I got legs," I reminded her, my mouth between her neck and shoulder. "The fucking you against a wall test."

"Con, anyone can walk by and see." She glanced nervously at the floor-to-ceiling window covering nearly the entire wall. The hallway on the other side was mostly empty since it was still early in the morning, but there would be the occasional client, doctor, or physical thera-pist milling about.

"Let them see," I rasped against her neck before sucking the tender skin there. "Or let's make it fast."

"Con..." she moaned a weak protest as I sucked on her earlobe, my hand kneading her soft breast as my hips rolled against her.

"Tell me something," I whispered, kissing the column of her throat. "Was I dreaming or did you fuck someone in bed next to me last night?"

Her red face and shocked expression told me everything.

"Razvan," she admitted.

"That sneaky. Fucking. Dragon." I punctuated each word with a thrust of my rock solid shaft against her clit. "Thinking. He can hoard. My pussy. Right. Next to me?"

"Wait." Her eyes widened. "Are you really mad about that?"

"No." I kissed her lips to reassure her. "But I'm going to fuck you so hard, he won't get a chance to do that shit again tonight."

"Connor." Her eyelids fluttered, and I knew she was torn between giving in to her pleasure and keeping the rational side of her brain. "I need to tell you something else."

"I'm listening, baby." I kissed her neck some more to tease her, but stopped my thrusts. She hesitated, and I pulled away to look at her, realizing this was serious. "What is it, Mel?"

"Um," she chewed her lip nervously. "Remember the last time we had sex? When Hunter and Raz first got together?"

"Yeah. What about it?"

BZZZZT!

Of course, my phone chose that moment to go off. I pulled it out of my pocket to silence the call, but Mel grabbed for it.

"Wait! It might be my sister."

"Shit. Sorry, babe." I handed it to her, and she answered, hitting the speaker button as well.

"Hello?"

"Hello, may I speak to Melody, please," a crisp woman's voice came from the phone.

"Melody speaking." She glanced up at me nervously.

"This is Angela Dyer from the investor's board at the Vaudeville Theater Company. I'm calling in regard to your audition yesterday."

5

MELODY

I stared at the phone, unable to talk due to my throat feeling closed up. *Shit!* In the midst of everything since last night, I had completely forgotten about my audition. I certainly didn't expect them to call back so soon.

"Are you still there?" Angela asked. From her sharp, no-nonsense tone, I could only gather she was the woman in glasses who seemed wholly unimpressed by my and Raz's audition.

"Oh, yes! Sorry, I'm here," I answered.

"Is this a good time?" Her crisp voice was jarring over the phone speaker.

"Yes! I'm sorry. I just uh, didn't expect to hear back so quickly." I settled on the bench while Connor remained standing. "What can I do for you?"

"After reviewing your audition with the other investors, we decided to go with a different act for our local theater," she informed me robotically. Yup, she was definitely Uptight Glasses Lady.

"I see..." My heart sank. Of course, it was a rejection call. Raz and I performed our hearts out, and she didn't even smile at our audition.

I really wanted that gig. Even though we had it good now with a house and plenty of land, Connor might not need the services of the FDR Center forever. We needed to plan toward the future, and I needed every dollar I could scrape together to get Jeanie and my younger siblings out of that trailer. They deserved so much more than struggling to adulthood like I did.

"Well, thank you for the call," I said, now eager to get off the phone.

"However, I do have another offer if you're interested," Angela continued.

Connor, who had been pacing around the room on his new legs, suddenly stopped and turned to look at me, his eyes wide and bright.

"Oh. Uh, yes?"

"A brand new Vaudeville Theater location will be having its grand opening next week. The performers we initially booked have broken their contract to chase another opportunity." Her monotone voice was laced with irritation. "If you are able to make it to the opening, we'll simply fill you in for the existing contract. Frankly, we don't have time to draft a whole new one for you."

"Oh! Uh, okay." I ran a hand through my hair, feeling drastically out of my element. "Where is the location?"

"Miami, Florida."

Connor cleared his throat and leaned in close to the speaker. "Good morning, ma'am. My name's Connor Shaw and I'm Melody's booking agent. Would you be so kind as to outline the terms of the contract?"

"Certainly," she quipped. "We'll pay a flat fee of thirty-thousand dollars for opening night to be divided among the performers at their discretion. Additionally, we'll also pay ten percent of ticket sales for the event."

My hand slapped over my mouth to prevent anything stupid from coming out while Connor and I exchanged wide-eyed stares. That couldn't be right. Thirty-thousand dollars?! I never imagined I'd see that much money in my lifetime, let alone on a single night.

"I see," Connor replied, keeping his voice calm. "So this is a one-night only event, correct?"

"Yes, although depending on the success of the show, we may offer more long-term contracts in the future."

"I see," Connor repeated. "We'll definitely take this into consideration. By when do you need our answer?"

"As soon as possible," Angela said. "If I don't hear from you by the end of the day tomorrow, I'll have to pass the offer onto someone else. We *need* performers for this show as this has been a highly anticipated event and we're nearly sold out of seats."

"We'll have an answer for you before then," Connor lifted his eyes to me. "May I have a copy of the contract so we can look it over in greater detail?"

"Certainly. I'll email it to you."

Connor gave her his email address and then we both said goodbye as I ended the call. We both leaned back and just stared at each other while the information sank in.

"That's a lot of money." I broke the silence first.

"A *shit ton* of money," he agreed, rubbing his jaw. "This must be one fancy-ass theater."

"The one Raz and I went to was super-fancy," I said, remembering the massive chandelier, plush seats, balconies and private boxes, and that huge stage we auditioned on. "What do you think I should do?"

"Take it," he said with no hesitation. "I'm no lawyer, but I'll look over the contract for anything crazy. But damn, thirty grand for one night? There is not much I would say no to for that amount of money."

"Same," I agreed. "But all the way in Florida?"

"Where I went to college," he grinned. "And in Miami, at the very fucking tip of Florida. It'll be a drive, but we can do it, babe. Especially for 30K."

"We?" I lifted my eyebrows. "So you're coming with me if I say yes?"

"Hell yes, I am." He slid his arms around my waist, nudging my legs apart to stand between them. "Anywhere you go, I go."

"Babe, you haven't been on stilts in weeks," I warned. "You still have to get these legs adjusted."

"I'll practice. They already feel tons better than my old ones, so they shouldn't be a problem." He dropped a kiss to my forehead. "Raz will go with you, too. Arjun probably won't, but whatever. He can house-sit. As for Hunter, jury's still out on that one, but even with just us three, it'll be a hell of a show. "

I stared up at him. "Do you really think we can pull it off? Do you think we're worth that much money?"

"Baby," he cupped my face, his forehead on mine, "just you alone are worth so much more than that. You're priceless."

"To you, maybe." I wrapped my hands around his forearms, my eyes lost in his. "But to thousands of strangers who've never seen me before? When my only worth to them is my entertainment value?"

"We could ask any random person who's seen you on stage before," he said, "and I'm positive they would say the same thing. You have an impact on people, and not just those of us lucky enough to have your love."

"I don't understand it," I said with a slight shake of my head. "I definitely don't see it like you do. I feel like a different person onstage. Is it because of my shaman powers or is that really *me?*"

"They're one and the same," he insisted, directing my gaze back to him.

"I wouldn't have that kind of presence if it weren't for—"

"I don't believe that for a second," he cut me off. "I don't know anything about all this magic shit, but what I do know is you're such an incredible person. Personally, I don't think it matters one bit whether some guy gave you a gift or not. You've always had a gift."

He pulled his face away to look at me. "You became a mother figure when you were just a child yourself. You stepped up and protected your siblings like a shield, even if it damaged you. And the moment you could save yourself from hell, you did."

"I feel like I gave up on them by leaving," I admitted.

"You didn't." His hands lowered to my shoulders, where he gave an affectionate squeeze. "To give up would've been to stay, to keep perpetuating that cycle. Do you realize how brave it is to break away from that? Do you have any idea how strong a person has to be? Your environment could have broken you, but it made you this strong, resilient, amazing woman instead."

I didn't know how to respond. Even after spending all this time with him and the other guys who showered me with love and adoration, I didn't feel like anything special. Maybe my brainwashing of being told I was worthless growing up still had a hold on me, but it was hard seeing his words as truth.

"What I'm trying to say is," Connor said, wrapping his arms around me and pulling me into his chest. "You can absolutely do this. You're ready, you're worth it, and you've been through hell and back. You can do any fucking thing you want."

6

MELODY

On the way home, Connor walked beside me with his new, long strides. He almost got away with leaving the wheelchair at the FDR center until I insisted on bringing it with us. The doctors' orders were to not overuse the new prototypes, so I'd make damn sure he didn't.

"Hey babe," he shot a naughty grin at me as the house came into view. "Get in the chair and I'll push you the rest of the way."

"No way!" I shot back. "You'll go super fast like a maniac."

"What happened to the girl who loved scary rides?" he teased, swatting my ass as he pushed the empty chair in front of him with the other hand.

"Even the scariest rides have safety features," I replied. "But nothing will stop me from falling out of that thing and getting trampled on if you come to a sudden stop."

"I won't do anything that would hurt you," he said, his

voice tinged with offense. "Promise. I won't even go that fast. I just want to see how well these legs can bear weight and resistance."

"Fine," I sighed, taking a seat in the chair, gripping the armrests and setting my feet up on the footrests.

Connor moved behind me, and I felt him grip the handles on the back of my chair. "Ready?"

"Not real-*aaahhh!*"

The damned liar took off like a fucking sports car. I heard his feet crunch on the gravel path like he was sprinting for a gold medal. The whole chair rattled as the world rushed by, as did my teeth, while I held onto the armrests for dear life.

"C-c-c-c-Conner! S-s-s-stop!"

"You'll fall out if I stop!" he laughed behind me.

Just as the house came rushing up to us and I was afraid I'd crash right into that beautiful wraparound porch, he gradually slowed until we came to a walk, and then a complete stop in front of the first step.

"Don't look at me like that," he said in response to my expression upon getting out of the chair and turning around to glare. "That was fun. Admit it."

"It would be more fun if I wasn't close to dying."

"But you still had fun."

I had a terrible poker face and couldn't keep it up. My glare cracked and the damn treacherous smile shined through. Yes, that scared me to death, but it was a thrill and a half that I hadn't felt in a long time.

"See! I knew it." He leaned across the chair to kiss me, then lifted each of his knees to examine his prosthetic feet. "These things really are crazy, though. They grip and push off the ground like real feet. Most of the power came from my quads but these puppies did an awesome job of assisting."

"Remember why we brought this thing in the first place," I said with a hand on the chair. "I know you want to push to the limit but no overdoing it, seriously. You should probably take those off soon for a break."

"Yes, ma'am." He leaned down for another kiss, this time pulling me around the chair and crushing me to his chest. Damn, I missed him doing that.

"Hey," he said when our lips parted. "What did you want to tell me? Before the phone call?"

Shit.

"Oh, yeah. Um..." I'd been working myself up to telling him all morning, finally found my inner lady-balls and just about did it when that phone call fucked up everything. Now this job was the only thing on my mind and I didn't have the mental focus to deal with that and a possible pregnancy scare. Shit, shit, shit.

"It's not important right now," I forced a smile. "We'll talk about that later."

He lifted a skeptical eyebrow. "You sure?"

"Positive." I swatted his ass, enjoying that it'd be up for grabs and not parked in a chair all the time now. "Let's tell everyone the news."

"Maybe not everyone," he muttered, following me inside. "Just the ones who need to know."

We had nothing to worry about in that regard. The house was silent and empty, the complete opposite of the crowd we had this morning.

"Where the hell is everyone?" I wondered, wandering from room to room.

"I see Raz and RJ," Connor pointed out the sliding

glass door to the back deck, where the dragon and tiger shifter hung out in the backyard.

"No Hunter?" I asked, jogging to catch up. It didn't matter if he had feet or wheels, my Marine was always speeding ahead.

"No wolves in sight, babe."

Raz and Arjun talked quietly near a tree, the same one he taught me to throw knives at and fucked me against like an animal. I grinned at the memory. Raz seemed to have the same idea, smirking and shooting me a wink as we approached.

"Nice legs, mate." Arjun gave Connor an appreciative nod as we joined them. "I'm sorry. There's no way to say that without sounding homosexual. Believe me, I've been trying to think of something since you came outside."

"Thanks, RJ! Pretty sexy, aren't they?" Connor spun in a circle, then did a goofy catwalk strut, much to the guys' amusement.

"Goofball." I rolled my eyes and nestled into Raz's side, where he slid an arm around me and kissed my temple. "I have news," I said, lifting my eyes to his. "The Vaudeville called me back."

"Oh?" His eyebrows lifted. "What did they say?"

"We didn't get picked for the local show, but they want us to do a grand opening show for a different location," I paused, "in Florida."

"Fuck Florida," he spat. "That was where I first landed in the US. I'll be happy to never set foot in America's swampy asshole again."

"Wait 'til you hear about the money, Raz," Connor chuckled.

"Thirty-thousand dollars," I said. "Plus ten percent of ticket sales. For *one* night."

His mouth fell open, then promptly shut again. "Guess I should've held my tongue," he said sheepishly.

"You don't have to come with me if you hate it so much," I said earnestly. "I don't want you to—"

"*Steluţa*, are you kidding?" His arm tightened around me. "If you're jumping on this, of course I'm coming with you."

"But you just said—"

"It's America's swampy asshole, I know," he chuckled. "But that's *a lot* of money. You can get all your siblings out of that hellhole for that much, easily." He cupped my face, staring inquisitively down at me. "You *are* going to accept this offer, right?"

"I don't know," I admitted. "It's... a lot to think about. Yes, the money's tempting, but it's *next week*. Can we put together a show worth thirty-grand in that time? And we'll be leaving the FDR center so soon after settling in."

"You know, for such a powerful shaman, you do lack a lot of self-confidence." The observation came from Arjun, who returned my narrow-eyed glare with a passive stare.

"This doesn't concern you, but thanks for your input," I snapped. "It's not like I don't have enough on my plate already."

"Arj, now's not the time," Raz added. "She's got a lot to think about."

"The hell do you mean, this doesn't concern me?" Arjun kept his gaze focused on me, ignoring Razvan. "You brought me into the Brady Bunch here, Mel. What, you don't want my input because we haven't fucked?"

"It's got nothing to do with that," I hurled back at him. "You've made it clear you don't approve and want no part in any ongoing carnival business, so why should I listen to your opinion?"

Arjun rolled his gaze skyward, chewing his lip and crossing his arms as he let out a long sigh. I fought to ignore how hot and flustered just looking at him made me feel. God, I hated how much his words got under my skin.

"Look, if you're so concerned about putting on a show that's worth the dollar amount attached to your contract, I'd be willing to go, too. Not that you need me to increase the perceived value."

He could have slapped me across the face and it wouldn't have shocked me as much. I just stared, dumbfounded. Connor and Raz said nothing, so I only imagined they were as dumbstruck as me.

"You can't be serious," I breathed. "You can't mean—"

"Look, I hate fire, alright? But what I hate more is being fucking caged for days on end and starving on old roadkill." He nodded at Raz. "Lizard boy here knows how to keep his flames cool enough to not burn me, as long as I'm careful. And seeing how all these wankers adore you, I can only assume you don't treat them like, well, circus animals."

"Why?" I asked with a slow shake of my head. "Why would you put yourself in that environment again?"

He shrugged. "Why did Hunter?"

"Because I rescued him. And his kids."

He inclined his head toward me. "There you have it."

"Arjun," I breathed, my thoughts whirling too fast in my brain for me to catch up. "You don't have to—"

"I know, Mel," he sighed, as if exasperated. "You made that clear. I have a choice. I don't have to help you. I also know I'm a cheeky bastard and it's hard for me to properly express myself. So let me just do this, please."

A silent pause passed between us like we were the only two people present. His eyes glowed with an unnatural beauty against the dull, muted colors of the forest.

"Okay," I said finally. "Thank you, Arjun."

"I quite like Florida, actually," he quipped lightheartedly, shooting a grin at Raz. "Reminds me of some of the forests in India where my mum's from. Much warmer and less dreary than London."

"You'd hate Romania, then," Raz muttered. "Damn, I'd fucking love to feel cold mountain air again."

"Well, look at you, babe." Connor beamed at me with pride. "We just might put on a million-dollar show yet."

"Let's aim for the modest goal of thirty-grand first," I scoffed before looking back up at Raz. "Hey, where is Hunter?"

"Who knows," he said with the undertone of an annoyed growl. "The whole pack took off again soon after you two left. They're out here somewhere, doing whatever wolves do."

I leaned my head on his shoulder and he kissed my forehead sympathetically. Disappointment washed over me as I looked through the dense trees, not a wolf in sight. What he told me this morning already felt like empty words. Maybe it was an overreaction, but it already felt like he was choosing his wolf family over us. Over me.

They were his original family. Before he ever met you, they would always come first, I reminded myself.

Still, it didn't shake the feeling that I was slowly losing Hunter. And what if, after this grand opening in Florida, they wanted us to stay and do more shows? What if we never came back here?

One thing at a time, Mel.

The four of us slowly walked back to the house. Connor brought up the contract from Angela on a computer and looked over it with a fine-toothed comb. When he felt confident there were no loopholes or pitfalls, I called Angela back and confirmed we would accept the job.

"Great!" she chirped over the speaker, the most emotion I heard from her yet. "We'll start advertising the new lineup right away. Will you need accommodations?"

"Um, yes?" Less than a week in this house and I already felt spoiled by having a wonderfully spacious master bedroom. I didn't want to go back to sleeping in the RV, even if it was just for one night.

"We'll set you up in the hotel down the street. How many rooms?"

"Um. Two, please. How much will that be?"

"It's on us, Melody. Remember, we're investing in you."

That last sentence caused a jolt of panic to surge through me. If a thirty-grand paycheck wasn't enough pressure, the expectation of being an investment sure was.

"Oh, right! Thank you," I replied, not wanting to give off the impression that this treatment was completely alien to me.

We finished the call and the four of us began brainstorming a show and choreography around the kitchen table. Connor ordered pizzas, and we practiced into the afternoon and evening. As each hour passed with no sign of Hunter and the pups, the feelings of disappointment and being let down ate away at me.

I tried to throw myself into the routines, imagining myself onstage before a massive ballroom full of people. I imagined their energy, their screams, cries, gasps, and thunderous applause as I led my men through their acts. The stage, as volatile and terrifying as it was, was my second home. I craved it again, the chance to tell stories and exhibit the talents of my acts without exploiting them.

But my vision didn't feel complete without Hunter.

It wasn't like I needed him as a half-shifted Wolf Man for a good show, I just missed him being here. I wanted his support, to see his sexy smile again. I wanted to see him and Raz being cute together, either with me in the middle or not. Like me, my dragon periodically looked to woods, letting out a small displeased sigh when no wolves emerged.

We called it a night long after the sun had set and only Razvan's fire illuminated the darkness. Stumbling upstairs on tired, shaky limbs, we said goodnight to Arjun, who muttered something about sleeping for fifteen hours and I didn't think he was joking.

Connor, Razvan and I showered together in the massive walk-in shower in the master bathroom. While they enjoyed soaping me up and I returned the favor to them, we were all too tired for anything especially naughty.

It was just before midnight when we settled into the king-sized bed, the entire house still and quiet.

"Damn wolf's gonna get an earful from me when he

gets back," Connor muttered, his voice vibrating against my cheek on his chest.

Raz muttered an agreement as he snuggled against my backside.

I only hoped Hunter's return would be a matter of *when* and not *if*.

7

MELODY

I couldn't place exactly what woke me up. The bedroom was pitch black, and both Raz and Connor's chests fell and rose with deep, even breaths.

Then a sound.

It was so faint, I couldn't even discern what it was. But it came from downstairs.

Now wide awake, I slid out of bed, careful not to disturb my sleeping men as I pulled on a tank top and pajama pants.

A light was on in the kitchen as I crept down the stairs. Soft, rustling noises and the clink of silverware floated up to me. I rubbed my eyes and blinked to force my eyes to adjust.

"Hunter?"

He looked up at me, gorgeous as ever. His hair was disheveled like he hadn't brushed it in a day or so. Those golden eyes looked wild, more feral and animalistic than I'd ever seen before.

"Hey little fox," he greeted me in a hushed voice. "What are you doing up?"

"Where have you been all day?" I ignored his question as I approached him, my body physically aching for his touch.

"I'm sorry," his face fell. "We went with Colt and Gabe to visit their shaman. I didn't expect it to go on all day."

"Why?" I folded my arms in front of my chest, suddenly feeling the most insecure I ever felt since dating multiple men. "What did you do? You have a shaman right here."

"Mel, it wasn't like that." He closed the distance between us, his hands on my bare arms. "I went to learn more about you. Maybe I could find out something that would help you decipher between your powers."

"Arjun's already started on that," I answered tersely. "I have Sight, Sense, Semblance, and Speak."

"I see." His mouth ticked up, my attitude having no effect on him. "Miriam doesn't have Speak. She's nowhere near as gifted as you."

"Hunter, I missed you." My arms flopped down to my sides, my voice taking on a whiny tone, but I didn't care. "So much happened today, and I didn't get to share any of it with you."

"I'm sorry, little fox." He cupped my chin, pressing a kiss to my mouth that I couldn't help but return, despite not wanting to. His kiss was like precious water I'd been thirsting for. "I really am. I'm not trying to neglect you. We're just trying to make up for lost time. The pups are ecstatic to spend time with their uncles again and I don't want them to miss out on that bonding."

"Even though one of them hates humans," I remarked.

Hunter let out a tight-lipped sigh and I could see the conflict in his face.

"Gabe is harboring a lot of pain, a lot of resentment, but he's coming around. I can tell he likes Miriam more than he'll admit. He's a proud, stubborn wolf."

Before I could reply, he scooped me up in his arms and carried me toward the theater room, where he settled us down on the loveseat.

"Now tell me everything that happened today," he said, his lips ghosting across my forehead. "I missed you too, little fox. So much."

I began, reluctantly at first, talking about Connor's new prosthetic legs and how much better they were than the old ones. He didn't have stilts in this house, but still did some impressive acrobatics while we practiced. When I got to the phone call and the money we'd earn, I almost forgot about being annoyed with him.

"Mel, that's amazing!" He kissed me hard, golden eyes beaming. "I knew you and Raz could pull it off."

"Hunter," I voiced his name softly. "Will you come with us?"

His face fell again, and I quickly rambled before he could answer.

"Not to perform. I'd just love for you to be there. Connor and Raz, and now Arjun, I guess, are such a storm. You're the calm in that storm. I need you to keep me sane while those three drive me crazy." My hand trailed from his shoulder down the center of his chest. "I miss you, Hunter. I miss... just being with you."

"I miss you too. I swear to God, Mel, I was thinking about you all day today. I hate being away from you for so long." He hesitated and my heart dropped into my stomach.

"But?" I prompted.

"But I should probably stay here," he finished. "I'll be thinking about the kids constantly. I'd rather not drag them along. They want to spend all their time with their uncles, but I don't want to be away from them, you know? Even if it's just for a night."

I nodded my understanding, even though it hurt.

"There's a possibility," I added. "That they'll want us for more shows if the grand opening goes well. If they offer that, we'll probably say yes. It'll be more money for my siblings, for whatever therapy Connor needs and such."

"And that would involve living in Florida permanently." He said aloud what I didn't dare to. It was getting too far ahead of myself but a strong possibility all the same.

"Yes," I confirmed.

I waited for him to repeat what he told me so emphatically this morning, that he would always choose me. That he wouldn't hesitate at all to bring himself and those kids, who I almost began to love as my own, to Florida or Timbuktu or wherever the hell I ended up. The fact that he was just one of three men I loved didn't even matter. I needed *him* and what only *he* could give me.

But he didn't.

"It's so fucking hard," he said instead. "As much as I'd love to follow my heart, to follow you to the ends of the earth if need be, I can't do that, Mel. I have to think of what's best for Roo and Rinna."

"And what is that?" I asked, my voice threatening to crack.

"I don't know," he admitted, resting his forehead on

mine. "They love you. Rinna wanted to start calling you Mom. But with their uncles here... I've never seen them so happy. Not since before we were captured."

He pulled me tight against him, his arms bracing against my back and pressing me to his chest. "Please know, this is the hardest decision I've ever had to make. Not even my mate dying did this to me. I love you, my little fox, so fucking much. More than I ever loved her. Please don't ever doubt that. Even though you're not a wolf, I know in my heart you were meant to be mine."

"Then come with us." My arms circled around his neck. "Bring the kids. Bring your brothers, too. I don't care. I just don't want to be without you—all three of you."

"Oh, Mel," he whispered gruffly. "I want to, so badly. But my brothers found home in these woods. They've been cut off from the rest of the pack, so it's just them and their shaman now. If I were to take the kids and go with you... I'd be separating my family all over again."

"We're your family, too."

"I know. That's why this is so hard."

His mouth fell to mine, and I kissed him with every fiber of my being. Every kiss was a plea, a desperate cry for him to choose me. I couldn't force him to make the choice. I wanted him to *want* to follow me with those two kids in tow.

I wanted him to forget his life before being captured, as selfish as that was. The carnival became such a turning point in all of our lives. But if I couldn't fully let go of my life before, what right did I have to ask him to do that?

I clung to him only more desperately as he laid me out on the loveseat, settling his weight on top of me while his hands roamed under my tank top. His touch was sweet, sensual fire, and I craved him even more, trying not to think it could be one of our last times together.

Clothes peeled away as I sensed the need in both of us to hold on, to cling to what we knew and enjoyed so much. We didn't want to face the unknown even if it was best for those most vulnerable among us—Roo and Rinna.

His hot flesh pressed flush to mine, his mouth on my neck as my fingers sailed across the length of his back—we wanted to be selfish, to hold on to this and savor it because we knew it couldn't last forever.

He pulled his hips back, holding the side of my thigh as he aligned himself and pressed forward—filling me up and splitting me apart at the same time.

A whimper escaped my lips at the first penetration, not because it hurt, but because it was almost *too* good. I realized this was our first time truly alone together without the other guys involved. I pressed my feet into the cushions and lifted my hips to meet his, wanting to savor every inch of contact.

"I love you, Mel," he groaned as he surged deeper. "I'll always love you, even if I don't have you."

"Then come with me," I panted. Tears prickled at my eyes and my nails dug into his back as the first jolts of a building orgasm shot through me. "If you love me, don't leave me."

"You're the one leaving," he said with a dry laugh. His fingers dug into my hips, the impact of his cock pressing me down hard into the loveseat cushions. "Stay. Don't leave, my love. Stay with me."

"I can't." My whole body seized up as the orgasm rocked through me, my thighs pressing to his sides and my arms locked around my wolf as if he would disappear at any moment. "You know I can't."

He slowed his thrusts, pushing up to his hands as he gazed down at me beneath him. God, he was so fucking beautiful. And he was *mine*, but for how much longer?

He looked almost ghostly in the darkness. Pale and flushed, breathing raggedly with exertion, his abs flexing on his long torso as he continued filling and emptying me. Loving and leaving me.

His hands traveled up the sides of my body, palming the curves of my waist, filling his hands with my breasts. Each touch was exploratory and intentional as his golden eyes took me in, like he was creating a memory to look back on.

He fell back down to kiss me when his hands cupped the back of my head, his hips picking up pace as he crashed against me. The tears I'd been fighting finally spilled when my next orgasm convulsed around him again.

He released with my name on his lips, and his fists locked in my hair. The tiny loveseat grew uncomfortable, but we stayed there all night, unwilling to let go.

8

RAZVAN

I woke up early and came downstairs to find Mel and Hunter entwined in each other on the loveseat. *Huh, looks like wolf boy came home after all.* I covered them with a blanket, then went into the kitchen for coffee and a bite to eat.

Not fifteen minutes later, I heard movement coming from the theater room and then watched as Hunter, with pants on but still shirtless, carried a blanket-wrapped Mel up the stairs. He treaded softly, careful not to wake her.

I regarded him as coolly as I could when he came back down, determined to not be distracted by his long, lithe muscles and ghostly pale skin. Mel may have let him off the hook, but not me.

"Morning, Raz," he greeted, trailing a hand against me on his way to the fridge.

"Wolf," I returned, stiffening against his touch. "Have a fun night?"

He stopped and turned to look at me, his face conflicted. At least he had the self-awareness to feel bad.

"No, honestly. Mel told me about Florida and everything. And I've been feeling shitty ever since."

"Poor you," I sneered. "Can't have your venison and eat it, too."

"It's not about me, Raz," he growled, his shoulders squaring up to me. At any other time, it would have been sexy. Now it just pissed me off. "It's about my kids. I can't uproot their lives and rip their worlds apart again. They need stability. You think I don't want to go? If I did, *then* I'd be having my venison and eating it too."

"So you'd rather raise them with your own kind, even with someone who hates humans?" I shot back. "You wolves and your pack mentality is just as bad as humans, I think."

"What, like you never hated humans at one point?" he retorted. "Like Arjun doesn't? Gabe is coming around, but he needs time."

"Too fucking bad. He's out of time. He doesn't get multiple chances to disrespect our shaman."

"I would *never* let him." Hunter stepped in close to me with a growl, his teeth already elongating. "I love her. I'll rip his throat out myself if he even looks at her like that again." With a blink, he paused and stepped back out of my space. "I don't think he would, though. I know you all don't trust him, but he's my brother. I know him. He knows not to mess with what's important to me."

I rubbed my jaw, debating for a moment to bring up what else was on my mind.

"What about us, then?" I wondered aloud.

His gaze flicked to my lips and then back to my eyes. "What do you mean?"

"Wolves don't look too kindly upon interspecies relationships, do they?" I crossed my arms. "How would your precious brothers feel if they knew about you and me?"

He let out a long sigh, dropping his gaze. "I don't know, Raz. It hasn't really come up yet. They're still getting used to having a shaman around and I've been trying to make them see not all humans are bad."

"Right," I scoffed. "And if we settle in Florida and you never see me or Mel again?" I spread my arms to the side. "Will you have your happy wolf pack with no regrets?"

"No," he breathed. "Any choice I make will have major regrets, Raz. I love Mel with all my heart. You mean the world to me, too. But they're my family, my blood—"

"Blood isn't everything," I countered. "You saw that with Mel's mother. I'd say the same for my own family. You, me, Mel, and Connor? That's the family we've made, the one we've chosen. Hell, Arjun's pretty much stuck with us too now."

I stepped in close, just like he did to me, my face inches away from his. "And if you won't kiss me in front of them? If you make excuses for them disrespecting the woman you love? If you use your own children as the reason to not follow where your heart wants to go? Are they really worth keeping around?"

A flash of movement out of the corner of my eye nearly made me turn my head, but Hunter caught my chin. He made me face him, eyes boring into mine for one passionate moment, then his mouth crashed to mine. Hard.

With a rough pull of my body against his, the sharp points of his teeth grew long and my cock did the same. I moaned, loving the pleasurable pain he gave me, and fisted his hair at the nape of his neck. Heat soared in my body at the wolf's taste and I fought to control my dragon's fire.

"Um, whoa. Okay."

Hunter slowly broke our kiss, but kept his forehead on mine. He turned his head to exhale a small plume of smoke that escaped my lungs and found its way into his mouth.

"Hey, little brother," he remarked casually, stroking a hand across my chest.

Gabe's eyes flitted between us, his face nearly as red as his hair as he tried to reconcile what he just saw.

"Uh, something you care to explain, Hunter?" he asked.

"No." My pale wolf smirked, turning back to face me as he planted a gentler kiss on the bridge of my nose. "Not really."

9

MELODY

The days leading up to Florida passed by too fast. We practiced day in and day out, perfecting a routine like we never had before. Arjun was surprisingly easy to work with. He made his usual sarcastic jabs but never complained about the boring, monotonous work of repeating his part over and over and over. If anything, it almost seemed like he enjoyed it.

We were so busy, I barely saw Hunter or the other wolves. They came and went as they pleased, sometimes bringing meat from a hunt, other times just stopping by the house to rest. Gabe never gave me any issue again. This morning, he even smiled when he said hello to me. But it wasn't his attention I wanted.

Hunter seemed to keep his distance from both me and Raz. Our dragon shrugged it off and acted tough, but I knew he was bothered by it, too. Hunter seemed happiest when focused on the pups. He rolled around on the lawn, wrestling and playing with them, laughing and smiling like any proud dad. But he seemed sad when he looked over at us.

He probably can't wait until we're gone, I thought bitterly. So we're not around to kill his mood and remind him of the choice he made.

I was lost in thoughts like those when I headed for the kitchen during a break—so much so that I ran straight into a hard chest I didn't recognize.

"Oh! I'm sorry, Colt." My face flamed as I looked up at the smirk of Hunter's older brother.

"Head in the clouds, Mel?" he asked, stepping aside for me. His voice was deeper than Hunter's, but other than that, he could have been a dark-haired, slightly older clone of my wolf.

"Nose to the grindstone is more like it," I chuckled, pulling the fridge open in search of something cold to drink.

"I've been watching y'all a bit," he remarked, leaning against the door frame. "Pretty impressive. I'm sorry we'll miss the main event."

I paused, my arm halfway out of the fridge with a can of Coke. We'd barely talked since we first met and I couldn't get a read on him. His expression didn't tell me if he was being genuine or sarcastic. I expected him to react like Arjun did initially when I auditioned for ringmistress—outraged that I'd keep performing with shifters.

"No need to look so frightened," he said with a smirk. "I'm a big bad wolf but I don't eat humans."

"I just couldn't tell if you were actually complimenting me or not." I shut the fridge and cracked open my can, holding his gaze.

"I was," he insisted. "Best of luck to y'all down there. I really mean that."

"Well, thanks."

He must have sensed my apprehension, because his smile widened as he folded his arms.

"I'm in favor of shifters doing whatever they want, as long as it doesn't hurt anyone. You've obviously given them the choice and are making sure they get paid and treated well, which is all you can do. My youngest brother may disagree but he's more of a pack traditionalist."

I couldn't stop what rolled off my tongue next. "Does your view include shifters of different species seeing each other?"

His eyebrows lifted slightly, but he seemed overall unsurprised. "You're talking about Hunter and the dragon shifter."

"Yes, his name is Razvan," I said defensively.

"You've got some bite, girl. I like it," he chuckled. "And yes. I see nothing wrong with interspecies dating. A few months ago, though," his voice softened, "I probably would have answered differently."

"Yeah, what changed?"

His gaze lifted away from me, focusing on something far away. "Miriam." He said her name in the same affectionate way my guys called me by my nicknames.

"Your shaman."

"Yes." His gaze returned to me. "She's changed everything. Not in a bad way, but," he ran a hand through his mane of black hair, "times are different now than how they used to be. We shifters *need* shaman. After years of trying to handle stuff on our own, we just keep getting killed and captured. We need humans on our side." His eyes shifted toward the window, where Roo and Rinna climbed all over Gabe like a jungle gym. "Some just aren't ready to face the reality of that yet."

"I'd like to meet Miriam," I said. "After Florida, I guess, but maybe we can—"

"I'll bring her by the house tonight," he said quickly.

"Oh," I blinked. "Uh, sure."

"You two would get along, I think," he said, leveling his gaze at me. "She's also had trouble fitting in with other humans." His brow furrowed. "Sorry. Hunter's told me a bit about you."

"It's alright." I waved it off with a smile. "Sounds like Miriam and I have a lot in common already."

WE WERE all winding down after dinner when Colt brought Miriam to the front door, but I sensed her before they even walked onto the property line. Her presence felt like a warm, dull pulsing in my veins, on a different beat than my own pulse. Before ever seeing her face, I knew she was powerful.

She wore a long maxi dress and walked in a way that made her look as if she floated over the ground. Long, dark hair framed vibrant green eyes and petite facial features. She appeared to be a few years older than me, maybe mid-twenties. Her skin tone was a medium tan, similar to Arjun's. The tiger in question stood from the table so suddenly, he knocked his chair over.

"Miriam!" he cried in disbelief. "What are you doing here?"

"She's our shaman," Colt answered for her with a protective growl.

"Your shaman was my stepdad's apprentice," Arjun shot back. "I haven't seen her since I was in London."

"It's good to see you again, little brother." Miriam finally spoke, her accent just as American as mine. She offered a small smile to Arjun. "What a small world it is. I hope you're well?"

"Better now than I was for the last four years," he muttered. "What brought you this way?"

"This is where I'm from," she answered with a light-hearted laugh. "I came back with Lhozen two years ago."

"Lhozen? He's here?" Arjun's eyes grew wide.

"Not here, but he's in the country." Her eyes flicked over to me. "You'll probably run into him at some point."

Remembering my manners, I stepped forward and cleared my throat. "Thank you for coming over, Miriam. I'm Mel. I've been eager to meet another shaman." I offered her a smile, which she returned. "We've just finished dinner, but did you want anything to eat or drink?"

"Just some tea, maybe. That's one of the things I've missed most about the U.K."

"I'll get that for you." Colt pressed a kiss to her temple, and I didn't miss the love and adoration sparking between them.

The guys cleaned up their dishes and slowly filed out of the kitchen to allow us girls to talk.

"So you've known Arjun for a while?" I asked, sitting across the now empty table from her with a cup of tea of my own.

Miriam wrapped her hands around her own mug. "We

were never that close," she said hesitantly. "I mean, I've always adored him but I don't think he's ever liked me much."

"Why's that?" I was surprised. Something about this woman made her instantly likable to me. Like she could be a real older sister, unlike the shitty one I grew up with.

Her eyes flicked up apprehensively to me. "His stepfather Lhozen took me as his apprentice not long after his mother was killed. I lived with them and Lhozen spent all of his free time training me. Arjun was unhappy about that. I think he saw it as his father replacing his mum with a much younger woman."

She reached across the table for my hand, her eyes practically begging me. "But it wasn't like that, I swear. Lhozen and I were strictly teacher and student. And he was a *hard* teacher. I think putting everything into teaching me was his way of grieving his loss."

"I believe you," I told her with a gentle squeeze of her hand. "And I'm sorry to hear Arjun judged you like that. But it must have been difficult for him too." A small twinge of envy passed through me. Arjun's mother must have loved him for him to miss her so much. I wondered what that was like.

"Yes, he was crushed. Poor thing." She gave a small shake of her head, then cast a curious look my way. "So he's in your harem, then? You've got a very good-looking group, I must say."

"Uh, not exactly." I laughed nervously, hiding my reddening face behind my mug of tea. "He has no interest in being one of four mates to a shaman, though he is helping me distinguish between my abilities. I wouldn't say we're friends but slowly warming up to each other, I guess."

"Oh, it'll happen." Miriam steeped her tea bag casually. "Has he told you about the variation of abilities from person to person?"

"No, it won't," I groaned, rolling my eyes. She and Connor should've started a matchmaking business with how insistent they were about this. "And no, he hasn't."

"A shaman's powers are as unique as the person carrying them," she explained. "It's like a fingerprint. No two shamans have ever been recorded having the exact same abilities." She spread her palms on the table. "We all have common threads, of course, and that is we can sense shifter-kind and have a better understanding of them. Just the way we're able to do that is always a little different."

"I have Sight, Sense, Semblance, and Speak," I told her. "Arjun told me that last one is rare."

"It is," she confirmed with a slight lifting of her brows. "Sight and Sense are fairly common, but Lhozen's grandmother was the last known one who could Speak." She leaned toward me and lowered her voice to a whisper. "I have Sight as well, along with a second type of sight."

"What do you mean?"

Her eyes lowered to her fingers stretched out on the table. "Your dreams are through the eyes of a shifter, yes? Usually in the past or in present time? My dreams are glimpses of the future."

"The... future?"

She nodded slowly. "I never remember it all, just random flashes and scenes. And it's always changing. Sometimes only in minor ways, like a single word being said, or the color of someone's shirt. Sometimes in huge, drastic ways." Her fingers squeezed around mine. "Do you want to know what I've seen about you?"

My head nodded yes before I could really think about it. Was this wrong or dangerous somehow, to know my future? I had no idea, but I felt the urgent need to know.

"You will be loved, happy, and fulfilled, Mel." A smile spread across her lips as her eyes lowered. "You and the baby."

My heart stopped as one hand jerked down to my stomach. *Shit!* It had been nearly a week, and I still hadn't told Connor or anyone. We were so busy all day and just collapsing into sleep exhausted at night. But yes, I was also completely chickenshit about bringing it up.

"Life will be good to you," Miriam went on. "But my dear Mel, you will go through Hell first."

An icy shiver went down my spine and I had a feeling she was being literal.

"You'll feel every ounce of their pain, hear the anguish in their voices, but you must remain strong for them," she went on, her hand squeezing around mine. "You must not succumb to it, Mel."

"Succumb to what? Whose voices?" I demanded.

"Lean on Arjun," she continued, as though I didn't say a word. "Your other men will try their best to help you, but they will not be what you need. You'll need Arjun the most."

❦ 10 ❦

ARJUN

The next morning's mood felt about as far from a sunny vacation in the Keys as one could get. Mel sulked. The white wolf looked depressed. Raz was pissy. And Connor was in a foul mood because Mel and everyone else was too. A goddamn chain-reaction of sourpusses. And people wondered why I didn't care to be part of a shaman's harem.

I stifled a yawn and choked down another cup of coffee. I hated the stuff, but apparently Mel and Miriam went through all the tea whilst chatting last night. I already couldn't sleep a wink after seeing my stepfather's mistress for the first time in years. Now she was becoming old chums with the shaman who saved my life. Just lovely.

Thankfully, Miriam was gone by morning, as were Hunter's brothers and the wolf pups. Despite only leaving for one night, apparently the pups would be too upset at seeing Mel leave. So Hunter employed his brothers to be a distraction and allow for some romantic goodbyes.

However, the tension in the kitchen was anything but.

Hunter and Mel barely spoke to or looked at each other. Raz did much of the same. I grew bored of this and wanted fresh air from the stench of coffee, so went out to the RV where Connor was checking it over for the long drive ahead.

"Need any help, mate?" I asked, approaching as he fiddled under the hood of the gargantuan vehicle.

"Hah," he scoffed. "Still awkward as fuck in there, huh?"

"How did you guess?" I groaned, scrubbing a hand down my face. "It's one night we'll be gone, two days max. I'm not sure I understand why they're acting like teenagers being apart for a whole summer."

"They're in love," he answered simply. "And there is the possibility of us staying out in Florida permanently, which puts a serious damper on things if Hunter insists on staying here."

"It's quite a big *if*," I remarked. "Really, what's the point of getting our knickers in a twist over what might or might not happen?"

"Again, love," Connor smirked, flipping over a wrench in his hand. "You act like you've never been in love before."

"I haven't," I answered truthfully. "Although I was engaged."

He paused in his work, looking me over quizzically. "So was I. The love part usually comes first, though."

"Arranged marriage," I sighed. "My mum grew up in a region of India where it's still common. Pretty old school by today's standards, but these traditional folks swear it's better that way."

"They still do that in Afghanistan. Shocked the shit of

out us American military kids," he chuckled. "So what happened?"

"I was captured and shipped over here," I shrugged. "Got thrown in a cage with a hotheaded dragon and the rest is history."

"Well, that's one way out of marrying someone you don't love."

We laughed together at that. The more I talked to Connor, the more I liked him. He was a good bloke.

He shut the hood of the RV, then jumped down from the bumper on his new robot legs. "She's all set to go. Now it's just dragging those two out of the house so we can get moving."

"Lovely," I groaned, but my complaint was premature.

Mel and Raz came around to the side yard with Hunter between them, the three of them talking quietly. Hunter paused, turned to Mel, and cupped her cheek before leaning down and kissing her passionately. She returned it with just as much reverence, wrapping an arm around his neck and holding onto him like she'd never let go.

A twinge of heat and something else ran through me, and I found myself looking away. This private moment wasn't mine to gawk at.

When I glanced up again, Mel had stepped to the side and now Hunter and Raz were wrapped up in each other. Seeing them together made me smirk to myself. Mum would have a fit, God rest her soul. She hated any kind of openly sexual deviance. Any time she complained about seeing same-sex couples together, I suggested she go back to India. I thought I was clever, but my tigress mother was not amused.

After their long, lingering goodbyes, Mel and Raz

trudged up the into RV with all the enthusiasm of children going to back to school.

"Y'all got everything?" Connor asked as he started up the engine. Those two just remained with their faces pressed to the windows.

"Remind me never to fall in love," I mumbled, taking the passenger seat and bucking myself in.

Connor just chuckled as he carefully drove the vehicle out of the side yard and onto the road. "That's a little dramatic, isn't it? Falling in love is a beautiful part of the human experience."

"If it makes you act like that? No thanks, mate. Give me a belly fully of meat, some tea to wash it all down, a place to sleep the day away, and I'm settled."

"Simple pleasures are great," he agreed. "But you're human too, bro. That big ol' human brain loves to make everything complicated. It's never satisfied with the simple things, not for long. Once you have everything you want, you always want more."

"Yeah?" I propped my feet on the dashboard and laced my hands behind my head, settling in for the long ride. "What do you want more of?"

"I'd like to go a whole three months without triggering my PTSD, for one." He lifted an eyebrow at me. "You've seen some shit too, RJ. Might want to get that looked at."

"That's where I'm thankful for my simpler cat brain," I answered. "Spending most of my time as a tiger made my years in captivity a simple predator versus prey situation. Sometimes I was one, sometimes the other."

"Animals experience psychological trauma, too. Even I know that, but fair enough," he replied. "Everyone processes it differently."

I ground my teeth in my jaw. Connor was not one to be underestimated. I couldn't be certain that he saw me snarl and turn when the occasional door slammed in the house. He certainly couldn't feel the spike of adrenaline rushing through me when Raz breathed fire during our practices. I made sure not to give any physical tells of fear, but Connor was especially perceptive for a human.

"And once you cure yourself of your own trauma?" I asked, returning the subject back to him. "What will be next?"

He lifted his eyes to the rearview mirror. I didn't see them, but Mel and Raz were silent behind us. Their scents intermingling—hers light and floral, his deep and smoky, indicating they were physically wrapped up in each other as well.

"It'll never be cured," Connor murmured in a low voice. "It'll always stay with me, but when I have it more under control, I don't want anything too crazy. Kids and a wife. You know, stability."

I stared at him as he drove. "And how do you expect that to work with... you know, all of you?"

He shrugged, smirking as he glanced over at me. "However my woman wants it to. I have my place with her and that's plenty enough for me."

"Mate, you're not even a shifter," I said with a shake of my head. "What's your excuse for being under her spell?"

"Ain't no spell, man," he answered. "It's just love."

THE JOURNEY TURNED long and uneventful. Raz took over driving after Connor started feeling soreness in his legs. I napped in the passenger seat, paced around the vehicle, shifted, then napped on the floor. This long drive was making me feel antsy and caged in again.

"RJ." Connor looked up at me from the small bed pushed against the wall. "Grab some Midol from the cabinet in the bathroom? Mel's got a killer headache."

He sat up with his back against the wall and Mel leaning against his chest. Her eyes were shut tight and her brow pinched as if she was in pain. His fingers moved in soothing caresses over her temples and forehead.

"Sure, mate." I retrieved the pain medicine and a bottle of water from the mini-fridge and handed them over.

Connor had her take a few pills with some water, kissing and murmuring to her as he rocked her gently in his arms. Just like when she was kissing Hunter, something uncomfortable and unfamiliar passed over me while I watched them, and I excused myself to return to the passenger seat.

"What's going on?" Raz asked from the driver's seat.

"Mel's got a headache."

"Hm." He glanced over at me. "You know how to drive this thing?"

"Fuck no," I shot back. "Connor's got her. Keep your eyes on the road."

His inked knuckles turned white on the steering as his lips pressed into a thin line. For fuck's sake, why did all of them want to rush to her side so badly? She had a bloody headache, not fucking gunshot wounds.

Another hour passed. My ears picked up soft whimpering from the back of the trailer, followed Connor's voice still trying to be soothing, but it carried an underlying tremor of fear. In the next moment, he took a few long strides up to us.

"Something's really wrong. We've got to pull over and find a hospital," he said, tapping Raz's shoulder.

"What's going on with her?" Raz made a sharp turn off the interstate at the next exit, too sharp for a such a large vehicle and we all struggled to stay upright.

"Careful, dude!" Connor barked. "I don't know, but her head is killing her and it keeps getting worse." He tapped my shoulder next. "Arjun, can you stay with her? I gotta give Raz directions with my GPS."

"Me?" I looked up at him, knowing he was dead serious because he didn't use my stupid nickname. "The fuck you want me to do?"

"Just sit with her so she's not alone." He smacked my shoulder more insistently. "Move it."

"Alright, Marine," I grumbled, rising from my seat reluctantly and moving toward the back of the vehicle.

Even my heart twinged at seeing Mel curled up in a fetal position, her hands pressed to her ears and her red face streaked with tears. Still, I knew nothing about how to comfort a woman in distress. I could charm women, yes, but that came from quick-witted banter and keeping an emotional distance. This vulnerable, nurturing stuff was not my forte.

"Hey," I said softly, lowering to sit on the mattress next to her. "Your guys are finding a hospital. You're going to be okay, Mel."

"Arjun, help me," she whimpered, thrashing on the bed like a fish out of water. "There's too many of them. I don't know how to make it stop."

"Mel," I choked out helplessly. "It won't be much

longer—"

"You don't understand," she sobbed. "You can't hear them."

"Mel, what—"

She grabbed my hand and pressed my palm to the burning, sweaty surface of her forehead. A sharp flash of sensation flooded over me so quickly, I almost thought I was on fire again. The feeling passed, then captured me again in an icy grip of pure horror.

I saw everything she saw, all in quick, vivid, and gruesome flashes. Cattle prods, whips, and batons. Fists, kicks, and BB guns. Cages, limping figures, and broken bodies. Weapons of every kind imaginable and the dozens of shifter species they inflicted upon.

I tore my hand away from her forehead and looked around for a place to vomit. Someone pushed a water bottle into my hand and I gulped it down, which helped settle my stomach a little.

"Did you hear them?" Mel asked in a weak voice. "Their screams. Some of them are barely alive."

I shook my head. "I could only see. You can hear too?"

She nodded, squeezing out a few more tears. "And I can feel... everything. In my body."

Just then, I noticed the red marks on her arms from where she had been scratching at herself.

"And it's getting worse?"

She nodded. "I've never felt it like this. Not even when I felt you." With an anguished whimper that tore right through my heart, she clapped her hands over her ears. "I don't know how to make it stop. I just want it to end..."

Before I could think of doing anything else, I slid my arms around her back and pulled her to my chest.

MELODY

I had never been in so much pain in my life. Not even when one of Mom's exes broke a bottle across my back and Jeanie spent the whole night picking glass shards out with tweezers.

What started as a simple headache not long after we left home turned into the most horrific visions in my head and sensations in my body. I wanted to jump out of the RV and prayed a semi-truck would hit me. It hurt so badly, but if I closed my eyes at all, what I saw haunted me.

"Listen to my voice," someone with an English accent said. Maybe Arjun? I had no idea if it was someone right next to me or one of the hundreds of voices in my head. "Focus on the sound of my voice and nothing else, Mel. You can do this."

I tried. Good lord, I tried. But the voice sounded like it was at the end of a long tunnel, and all the pain and abuse I felt was slowly dragging me away.

"I can't," I whimpered out. "You're too far away."

Hands touched me, some with gentle caresses and

others with fists. I wondered if this was what Connor's PTSD felt like, not being able to discern between reality and how my mind was just fucking me over.

"Stay with me, Mel. You're right here, love. You're in your own body. You are your own person. No one is hurting you. You're with me and your men. You're safe. Listen to me and focus on that."

The voice continued in a warm, soothing tone, and I tried desperately to hold on to it like a lifeline. But sometimes the screams drowned it out and I couldn't hear all the words.

I saw through the eyes of a small animal, shaking with fear in a dark corner. Humans dragged a struggling black bear with a chain around its neck. One of them pressed a handgun into the bear's shoulder and squeezed the trigger. The bear roared in anguish and tried to swipe at the human, but its other paw hung limply at its side. The animal I was seeing through, her cub, cried out a desperate plea and pressed against the bars of his cage, tiny paws swiping desperately at nothing.

"I can't stand this," I sobbed, forcing my eyes open to not witness more scenes of torture. "I don't want to see any of this."

My hands found a smooth, solid wall, and I scrambled closer to it. Then I slammed my forehead into the wall as hard as I could. I didn't want to die, just pass out. I was so desperate to get these images out of my head and I knew none of my guys would hit me in the head to knock me out. Sweet unconsciousness, please take me away from seeing and feeling all of this...

But then what if I still dreamed?

It didn't matter. I could only smack my head on the wall twice before someone dragged me away.

"No, please," I begged, feeling for the smooth, solid wall again. "I can't be awake. I can't do this."

"Listen to RJ, babe. You can fight this but we're not letting you hurt yourself."

Connor? Was he here?

"I'm right here, *steluța*. We're all right here. You're safe, my love. Come back to us."

"Raz..." I squeaked out, trying to make sense of the faces that morphed between my lovers and the cruel, hard faces of strangers.

The bite of a whip on my back felt like a kiss. A gentle caress became a closed fist punch to my gut. Everything bled over and between each other in blurry, dreamlike images. Jesus, when would it end?

A low rumbling started up, faintly at first, then growing louder and stronger. I saw through one of many caged parrots on a truck, and figuring it was the engine roaring. But it continued even when my vision shifted to something else.

The rumbling stayed constant, a repeating rhythmic noise that vibrated gently across my skin. I found it comforting and clung to it. After a moment, the visions faded. The windows and walls of Connor's RV slowly returned with full clarity. The sounds of torture faded away, as well as the pain, except for a dull ache in my forehead.

And the rumbling remained at its loudest volume yet, soothing like a balm to my sore brain.

"Jesus tap dancing Christ," Connor sighed. "You scared us to death, babe."

The rumbling nearly drowned him out. I could barely hear him and I was so tired now.

"What is that noise?" I murmured, rubbing my aching forehead. "It finally made everything stop but I can still hear it."

"Take a look and see, steluţa," Raz grinned. He sat on the floor in front of me, his hands resting on my legs. My dragon's eyes looked heavy and tired, but also full of relief.

I sat up from where I'd been reclining and looked behind me.

A massive Bengal tiger with the most striking blue-green eyes looked back at me. I had been leaning against his side, where I felt the deep rumble of his purr vibrate through me.

He continued purring, sounding like a small jet engine as he gazed back at me.

"Arjun," I breathed. "You saved me. I literally felt like I was dying several times."

Lay back down and rest, he thought to me. *The visions could come back while you're sleeping, so lean on me and I'll keep them away.*

He sounded so stiff and formal in my mind. I also realized for the first time that his accent didn't come through in my thoughts. But thinking about it too much made my head hurt.

"Thank you," I said. My eyelids drooped heavily, but I still reached a hand out. "May I touch you?"

His large head tilted as if confused by the question, but then pressed his forehead against my palm where I scratched him. My hand all but disappeared in the dense orange fur, my fingers barely stretching from one of his ears to the other. Those eyes closed slowly, as if in utter relaxation, and his purring volume only increased.

"I'll get you an ice pack for your head, steluţa." Raz rose from the floor and gingerly kissed me where my head throbbed. Shit, that was going to be a hell of a bump.

"Are you really okay with me lying down on you?" I asked Arjun. "I know we're not all that close—"

The tiger huffed, pausing his purring for a moment to shove me down against his side with his head and one large paw. I noticed how careful he was not to get his claws anywhere near me.

"Alright," I laughed, lowering my head to rest on the fur right above his ribs.

I curled my legs up close to me, shifting around a little to get comfortable before finally resting my hands near my face on Arjun's side. His purring immediately started up again, and he lowered his giant head to his paws.

My brain was too wiped out to think much about what just happened, but as I drifted off, cozy and secure against one of the most dangerous animals in the world, I mumbled, "Seriously, thank you, Arjun."

The tiger shifted slightly underneath me and I felt the tickle of his whiskers as he gently nuzzled my leg.

12

MELODY

I woke up to cold water dripping in my eyes.

"What the—"

As I moved to get up, that was when the melting ice pack tumbled off my forehead down to the blanket covering me.

I sat up, stretched, and tried to make sense of the world again.

Arjun still laid behind me, although his purring stopped. He breathed deeply, whiskers twitching slightly in his sleep. My eyes traveled over his form, taking in the beauty and strength of the tiger curled around me protectively.

He was beautiful in human form too, but up close the tiger seemed like such an otherworldly creature. Books and movies could never do justice to this powerful force of nature that was somehow related to the chubby tomcat that hung around my old trailer park.

The RV was quiet and still. A quick look up toward the

empty driver's seat told me Connor and Raz had gone somewhere.

I pushed the blanket away and swung my legs to the floor. My head no long throbbed, but a quick poke with my fingers told me I still had one hell of a bump. Hopefully, my top hat would hide it during our show.

A grunt behind me made me turn around. Arjun opened one eye lazily and then stretched, his claws the size of Raz's knives as they extended long on those paws the size of my head. He then lifted his head and yawned, his mouth big enough to swallow one of my legs whole.

"Good morning," I greeted groggily before blinking up at the light still streaming through the windows. "Or afternoon, whenever it is."

"Sorry to disappoint, dove," Arjun's mouth shifted back to human while he was still mostly a tiger, which was a little freaky to see, "but we did not spend a romantic night together, despite what your jumbled memory may tell you."

He finished his shift, then made a big point of covering his naked lap with the blanket, those blue-green eyes teasing me. The first time we ever truly spoke, he had just shifted and didn't have any clothes on. I did not want to deal with looking at a naked man I wasn't sleeping with, so refused to look at him until he got dressed.

Now, it was all I could do not to look at him. His warm, brown skin was unblemished except for a few burn scars on his ribs and arms. A light dusting of dark hair swept across well-defined pecs. Like Hunter, he looked built for swimming or long-distance running. A long, slender torso carved with abs that disappeared under the blanket in his lap. His musculature looked slightly bigger than Hunter's, though not as beefy as Connor, with arms and shoulders that looked powerful and swift.

"With you gawping like that, I'm starting to know what my prey feels like," he joked, poking me with an elbow.

"Fuck! Shit, I'm so sorry." I forced my eyes away as my face heated up like the sun. "I didn't mean to stare, I just zoned out. I'm still so out of it from before." A lame excuse, but still a plausible one.

"That was one hell of an ordeal," he remarked, the humor gone from his voice.

"My head just started hurting and then it all came on at once." I stared at my hands, remembering the tiny, helpless bear cub paws sticking through the bars of a cage. "It felt like dozens, maybe even hundreds of shifters coming through me at once. And all of them were being hurt, caged, or watching it happen to others. I've never seen anything so horrible."

"You are highly empathetic," Arjun stated matter-of-factly. "Have you always been able to feel what others felt physically? Even before you knew you were a shaman?"

I thought for a moment and nodded. "Yes. When I wasn't able to block my siblings from getting hit, I felt their pain when they cried. Not just the physical pain either, I could feel their heartbreak and confusion about it. Sometimes Mommy was nice to them, but other times she was so mean and they didn't understand why."

"Fuck me," Arjun muttered, his brow knitted as he listened. I remembered he didn't know my past like the other guys. He wasn't there when Hunter and I confronted my piss poor excuse for a mother.

I shrugged at his response. "It's just what I've always

known. When I was younger, I pretended I could absorb all their pain like a sponge so they couldn't feel anything. I don't think it really works that way, though."

"Unfortunately not," Arjun sighed. "Even so, many shaman have given themselves as martyrs for shifter kind. But the thing about martyrs is they're no good once they're dead." He gave me a stern look, his eyes resting on my forehead.

"I wasn't trying to kill myself," I said defensively. "I was just trying to knock myself out to make it stop. I didn't know what else to do."

"Well, it's a good thing you weren't near an open door," he remarked. "If you had jumped out while we were moving? All bloody three of us fools would have jumped after you without a single thought and this old bucket would have gone careening across the highway."

"Aww. I'm so flattered, Arjun." I mockingly batted my eyelashes at him.

He snorted in reply, folding his arms across his chest. "Just because I don't like to watch anyone suffer doesn't mean I'm in love. An easy concept for an eighteen-year-old girl to get confused."

"Oh yeah? How old are you?"

His lips twitched with the beginnings of a smile. "I'm twenty-two."

"See, you're not that much older than me." I propped my elbow on my knee and rested my chin in my hand, feeling like this was the most productive conversation I had with him yet. "Speaking of the men who are in love with me, where are they?"

"Getting food. And tea," he answered. "God, I hope

Razvan got through his thick head that I need English breakfast, not that Earl Grey bullshit."

"So when you talk about martyrs, do you mean you've seen that happen to other shamans too?"

"Well, every shaman communicates with shifters a bit differently," he began, running a hand through the black hair that began to fall in his eyes.

"That's what Miriam told me," I said. "Their abilities are as unique as a fingerprint."

He made an odd face at the mention of her, but nodded his head in agreement. "Right. My stepfather had episodes of overwhelming shifter visions that drove him to drink a lot. I still don't think he saw them nearly as vividly as you."

"My mom drinks a lot too," I replied, feeling a strange sense of solidarity with him. "Well, even a lot is an understatement. That's basically the reason I ran away and," I waved my hand through the air, "here I am."

As Arjun looked at me while I spoke, I felt a softness filtering in around him. Like he had always been slightly on edge, defensive and ready to strike if need be, but right then it gave way just slightly.

"Lhozen didn't get too bad until after my mum died," he said. "Then he was hitting a full bottle of Johnnie Walker almost every night when he wasn't sticking his sad, grieving prick in *her*."

I remembered Miriam's words to me, how she thought Arjun didn't like her, despite that she never got involved with his stepfather. She had probably tried to explain it to him before, so would it do any good to say anything now? From the way he spoke, he seemed utterly convinced that

Lhozen fell deep into drinking and this much younger woman immediately after his mother passed.

Honestly, I barely knew either of them and it didn't feel right to try to convince him that something he believed so deeply was wrong. Even if my gut told me Miriam was telling the truth.

"What happened to your mom?" I decided to ask instead.

"Poachers happened," he answered with a heavy sigh. "The only place we could shift in London was a wildlife park. Humans could still get buy entry and drive around like they were on safari or some shit. Mum and I spent a couple nights a week there, hunting, stalking, napping. Just getting the tiger out of our system, you know."

I stifled a giggle at the thought of using shifting as an excuse to take long naps. Such a cat shifter thing to say, not that I knew any other cat shifters.

"One day, this lot gained entry and smuggled guns in." His eyes took on a faraway look. "They were looking to get as many exotic hides and trophies as they could get away with."

"Fuck," I whispered. "Arjun, I'm so sorry."

"They got a rhinoceros, chopped its horns off and left it there bleeding," he continued. "Tusks from an elephant. A few ibex heads to mount on their walls. Skins from zebras and jaguars." He let out a long breath. "And Mum, of course."

"Jesus. How old were you?" I hardly dared to ask.

"Fourteen," he answered.

My hand reached out and took hold of his before I knew what I was doing. "That's terrible. I'm so sorry for everything you went through."

He looked at our hands clasped together as though he didn't know what to make of them, but didn't pull away. After a moment, his thumb slowly stroked over my palm.

"I could say the same to you," he replied.

13

RAZVAN

"Connor!" I craned my neck, looking around the store for the man with robotic legs. "Where the fuck are ya?"

"Ugh, language!" A middle-aged woman shot me a dirty look as she breezed by me, holding her wide-eyed daughter close to her body.

"What?" I glared at her. "I'm speaking English."

"There are children in this store, you brute! Watch your profanity!" Her eyes inspected my tattoos disapprovingly as she mumbled some bullshit about the devil and saving my soul.

I rolled my eyes, muttering a half-hearted apology while I looked around again. "Connor!"

"What?" he demanded, popping up out of nowhere and coming toward me with an armful of things to dump into the grocery cart.

"God bless you, sir! Thank you for your service!" The same bitch who gave me the stink-eye practically swooned as he walked past her. His dog tags were visible like usual, but so were his prosthetic legs, which he didn't normally show off in public.

"Thank ya, ma'am!" He shot her a winning smile, which immediately dissolved into a groan and an eye roll once he reached me. "She's the same person who would spit at me if I was sitting in the street with a cardboard sign. I guaran-fuckin'-tee it."

"Heh. Can you remember what fucking tea Arjun wanted?" I asked, making sure to make my *fucking* especially loud as I turned to the rows of boxes on the shelves.

"I dunno dude, just grab something."

"No, he wanted something specific. You know these English pricks and their *fucking* tea."

Smothering his laugh as we heard the woman's audible gasp in the next aisle over, Connor pointed to a box. "I think it's that one."

"Sure, whatever. Looks familiar." I snatched it off the shelf and threw it in the cart, eager to get back and see how my steluţa was doing. "If it's the wrong one, the big pussy will just have to deal."

After going through the ridiculously long checkout line —seriously, why did Americans buy so much damn food at once?—we made it to the RV, parked along the furthest row of spaces in the parking lot.

"*Steluţa,*" I breathed a massive sigh of relief when I saw she was awake and no longer seemed to be in pain.

"Hi, my dragon," she smiled at me.

"How are you feeling, my love?" I took her face in my hands and kissed the bump on her head. It already shrank considerably, but we got another large bag of ice for it just in case.

"Better," she murmured before her soft lips found mine.

I let out a groan at the sweet contact of her mouth, pulling her to me and kissing her like I hadn't seen her in days. Connor and I had been so worried, and so helpless to do anything for her. If Arjun hadn't been there and thought so quickly, who knew when her torment would have ended?

I paid him no mind on the bed next to her, easing her back down on the mattress with one hand cradling her head as I devoured her mouth. Even if he didn't want a taste of her, which I didn't believe for a second, he'd have to get used to seeing it.

Someone grabbed my shoulders forcefully and yanked me away from my woman. I turned with a growl when my lips disconnected from hers, nowhere near ready to be done kissing her.

But Connor, with his insane strength for a human, tossed me aside like a rag doll and took my place, his arms enveloping Mel and kissing her neck as she laughed.

"Wait your turn, asshole," I snarled, smiling despite myself.

"You had long enough. I was worried about her too, lizard boy." His voice was muffled against her skin. Mel looked up at me apologetically, but her smile was too wide.

I smirked back. Of course she would enjoy this, her men fighting each other over her.

"That's how it's gonna be, ah?"

I grabbed Connor's shirt in my fists and pulled up. He batted my arms away and went back to her, but I grabbed him around his middle and pivoted around, judo-tossing him to the floor.

"Nuh uh, man!" He rose to his feet quickly and shook his index finger at me. "I'm not Hunter, you can't do this gay wrestling shit with me."

"Aw, you're no fun, Con," Mel pouted adorably from the bed.

"You'll wait your turn then, robo-legs," I laughed, dropping back down to the bed beside her.

"Boys, you know there's plenty of me to go around," Mel giggled, stroking a finger down my cheek.

"Fucking neanderthals, the lot of you," Arjun muttered. He'd been scooted to the edge of the bed amid our skirmish and quickly pulled on a pair of pants before getting up. "Please tell me you got my tea, Raz."

"Mm," I mumbled distractedly as Mel dragged her nails across my scalp. "There's a sandwich for you," I told her. "Without a wolf, unfortunately."

"Thanks, dragon," she kissed my cheek, then leaned back and looked at me. "You miss him?"

"A little," I admitted. "A little pissed, too. I wish he'd get his head out of his ass and see what's right fucking in front of him."

"I can see his perspective though." She propped herself up on her elbows. "It's hard for him, choosing between what he wants and what's best for the kids."

"You're an angel to be so patient with him, and that alone means he should choose you."

"Us," she corrected me, stroking a finger across my lower lip. "Choose us."

"While this is all romantic and lovely," Arjun interjected, tea in hand like the English prick he was, "Mel and I need to work on putting up shields in her mind, lest she get hit by another wave of information like that."

"Yeah, what exactly was that?" Connor piped up, stirring up some instant coffee.

"I caught a glimpse when I touched her forehead," Arjun said, looking at me. "It looked a lot like the compound where they first held us, Raz."

"Fuck, those poor bastards," I muttered. "I can still hardly believe we got out alive and relatively unscathed. So many shifters died because of the horrible conditions or were injured badly to the point of being disfigured."

"There were so many children there." Mel curled her legs up to her chest. "I saw through the eyes of a bear cub as his mother was tortured."

I pulled her close and rubbed my hands down her arms, sensing the tremors through her body.

"What the fuck?" Connor's eyes darted between Arjun and I. "What the hell is this place?"

"Think of it like a distribution center," Arjun explained. "It's the first place we get dumped at after being captured. Hunter was probably in a similar place. We get evaluated, experimented on, all that lovely stuff before a price is put on our heads. Sometimes they hold auctions. Once someone buys us, we're shipped out to our new homes. Usually a circus, sometimes a zoo or a fucking foreign cosmetics company. Sometimes just a rich, sadistic fuck who likes owning a person who can turn into an animal."

"They're constantly crying for help," I murmured, tightening my arms around Mel. "You're probably the first person in ages who's heard them."

"Not only that. Remember, she can feel everything being inflicted on them," Arjun pointed out. "She needs to learn how to block it out, otherwise next time she'll have much worse than a lump on her head."

"Yeah, don't go doing that again, babe," Connor said. "I got enough brain damage for all of us."

"You guys are totally missing the point," Mel huffed, wriggling until I loosened my grip on her. "This trip isn't about the show anymore. Those shifters need us. I can't just ignore them after feeling their suffering like that."

"Lawd," Connor groaned, rolling his gaze toward the ceiling. "Jesus, you've blessed me with an amazing woman, but why in the Lord's name does she insist on saving everybody?"

"Because I'm a shaman." She leveled her gaze at him. "And it's the right thing to do."

"Wasn't talking to you, babe. I was asking Jesus."

"*Steluța*," I said while Arjun laughed into his tea, and Connor continued pleading with his imaginary god in the sky, "the compound is nothing like sneaking into a carnival. It's a massive warehouse with top-notch security. I'm talking armed guards posted twenty-four seven, cameras everywhere, only one way in or out. They see it as guarding millions of dollars worth of merchandise, so they're serious about keeping it secure."

"So?" Her warm brown eyes lit up with a fire I'd never seen in her before. "You're a fucking dragon."

"You flatter me, my love," I kissed her temple. "But you'd need a whole fleet of dragons to take on this place. And even if we just light her up, there's the matter of getting the shifters out safely and discreetly."

She sighed, leaning back against me. "We have to do something. Even if it's a long shot, imagine if we succeed. We could stop the shifter trade for good!"

"But if we fail," Arjun said, "Not only do Raz and I risk being enslaved again, we could lose one of the most powerful shamans alive."

"What do you mean?" Mel demanded. "They'll kill me?"

"Or worse," he replied. "They'll capture you too. And force you to use your abilities to control *us*."

14

MELODY

After more long hours of driving, night had just fallen when we reached our hotel in Miami.

"Oh my god, we're right on the beach!" I pressed my nose to the window, unable to believe I was looking at the real world outside and not a postcard.

"Let me guess, never seen the ocean, either?" Arjun teased. "I'm still not convinced you haven't lived under a rock your whole life."

"If by a rock you mean my morbidly obese, alcoholic mother, you'd be right."

He laughed softly at that, brushing past me with the lightest of touches on my waist. I froze in place, unaccustomed to this new affectionate side of him but not entirely hating it.

He spent the last few hours teaching me how to meditate, taking ideas from his Hindu upbringing and integrating them with lessons he saw his stepfather teaching other shamans. I got frustrated quickly, not seeing the point at all in sitting with my eyes closed and breathing, but he was surprisingly patient with me.

By the time we reached Miami, I could feel the presence of the shifters clouding my consciousness again. They came through even more vividly, like we must have been closer. My heart sped up and my stomach churned at feeling those wounds and thoughts again, but I remembered how Arjun told me to create shields in my mind.

"Use whatever imagery resonates the most with you," he told me. "Maybe a castle with walls surrounding it. An island surrounded by ocean where nothing can touch you. A wild sex party with all of your men, it's completely up to you."

I did use mental images of my men, but not in the way he suggested. The first line of defense in my shield was Connor, standing at attention like the proud Marine he was. He protected me from the first moment I ran into trouble at a carnival, so it made the most sense to me. To focus on my breath, I pictured Razvan breathing fire and imagined the strength in his lungs. What gave him life also gave him the power to destroy. To remember what I loved most, I pictured Hunter and the pups playing together, laughing and smiling. Love and protecting the innocent, those were the most important things, the reasons why I was doing this at all.

And if I ever lost focus, I pictured a Bengal tiger with blue-green eyes watching me with its silent wisdom. The guide and the teacher who pulled my mind out of a dark, hellish place and showed me how to defend myself.

Keeping these mental barriers firmly in place, I followed the guys out of the RV and into the fancy beach-side hotel. My fingers flexed with tension at my sides as the cool, salty breeze washed over us. There were tons of shifters in this city. I sensed all of them easily now.

My feet carried me stiffly into the lobby and I hardly dared to breathe for fear if I lost focus and my mind became consumed with suffering again.

"You're doing great," Arjun whispered with a gentle touch to my shoulder. "It gets easier the more you practice."

I didn't know he was still behind me, but mumbled my thanks as I followed Connor up to the front desk. As if sensing my discomfort, my Marine wrapped an arm around my shoulders and pulled me close with a kiss to my head.

Closing my eyes, I leaned into him with a shuddering breath. I dared to relax just a hair and my mental shields stayed up, thanks to my protective Marine.

"I'm sorry, we've overbooked and the two rooms held for you are no longer available," the woman at the front desk said after a few moments of typing on her computer.

"Ridiculous," Connor huffed in his fake manager's voice. "I'm calling Angela Dyer right now and—"

"Not to worry, sir. We've upgraded you to make up for the inconvenience," the woman said, not looking up from her screen. "You'll be in a suite but I'm afraid we only have one available."

"I suppose that'll do," Connor grumbled with a heavy sigh.

After receiving our room keys, Connor led us to the elevator like he knew exactly where to go. He practically skipped down the hallway as soon as we were out of sight of the front desk.

"Wait til you see this, babe," he grinned, kissing me. "Ever seen a hotel suite before?"

"I've never even been in a hotel room before," I answered. "What's the difference between a room and suite?"

"Check it out." He swiped his key card through the door and pushed it open, revealing what looked like a luxury apartment on the other side.

"Oh, my..."

I walked through breathlessly, feeling like I was in a dream. A floor to ceiling window with an amazing view of the beach, along with a spacious balcony and deck chairs. Marble tiles covered the floor with columns to match. The furniture was sleek, modern, perfectly coordinated, and spotless.

"It's not as big as our place," Connor slid an arm around my waist and dropped a kiss to my shoulder, "but there's a living room, kitchen, and two bedrooms. Arjun will still have his own room."

"Have you stayed here before?" I looked at him over my shoulder.

"Not here, but I rented a suite with a bunch of college buddies once. Like ten of us in one place like this, it was nuts." He spun me in his arms and kissed me long and deeply. "I've always wanted to pamper my woman by staying in a place like this. It might be on someone else's dime now but here we are, babe."

"Connor." I placed my hands on his biceps and broke off the kiss abruptly. I couldn't ignore it or hold back anymore. I already delayed things to the point of no return and couldn't afford to chicken out like this. Every day that passed without telling him just made it a bigger lie.

"What's wrong?" Those deep green eyes conveyed hurt as they bore into mine. "You don't like the room?"

"No, it's not that at all. I love it." I looked past him to see Arjun and Raz meandering from room to room, pointing out fixtures and talking softly to themselves. "Can we talk somewhere in private?" I asked, returning my eyes to Connor.

"Of course," he said immediately and pulled me to the nearest bedroom. It was relatively small, so probably not the master, but still had a gorgeous view of the ocean and its own bathroom that looked like a spa. "What's going on, babe?" he asked, seating us both down on the bed after shutting the door.

I clasped my hands in my lap to try to stop them from shaking. My heart felt firmly lodged in my throat and I didn't know if I'd be able to speak at all.

"I want to say I'm sorry first." I lowered my eyes to the bedspread, focusing on the embroidered palm trees. "You're probably going to be pissed, and it's completely my fault I didn't tell you this sooner, when we could have done something about it."

"Baby, you are the love of my life." He took my hands and brought them to his lips. "I could never be pissed at you. If you're struggling with something, all I want to is to be here for you. Now, please tell me what's going on."

"I think," I choked out, then swallowed and tried to take a breath. "I think I might be pregnant."

I didn't dare look up at him, but felt his hands squeezed around mine.

"Babe... you serious?" His forehead pressed gently to mine.

"We didn't use a condom last time, remember?" The words tumbled out like shaking leaves. "You always reminded me to be so careful before. And I just got so caught up in you, Hunter, and Raz... I wasn't thinking straight. It didn't even occur to me until later. I wanted to tell you so we could get a Plan B pill but then the theater called back and Hunter's brothers were there...."

"Shhhh." He quieted my ramblings by pulling me close and rubbing his hands up and down my back. "My silly, sweet girl. You don't have a damn thing to apologize for. It's just as much my responsibility as it is yours."

"You're not mad?" I looked at him to see a smile and bright green eyes staring back.

"Do I look mad?" His smile only widened, and his kiss that followed was full of giddiness and excitement.

"But you said before," I swallowed, "that you didn't want any, you know, accidents dragging us down."

"That was when our broke asses were living in the RV and I walked on legs that nearly killed me," he pointed out. "Now look at us, babe." He spread his arms wide to indicate the whole suite. "We're about to bring home over thirty grand for one show, and that's just the beginning." His arms dropped as he studied my face. "How do you feel about it?"

"I don't know," I admitted. "I'm relieved that you're not mad, but now it feels like I have so much to protect. The shifters here, my siblings. I was almost starting to think of Roo and Rinna like my own kids, but now I might have this one, too. I just want to keep them all safe and I don't know if I can do that."

"You're not alone," he told me solemnly, running a protective hand across my abdomen. I couldn't deny the rush of heat to my core at the thought of him as a father. A *real* father at that, and not just a sperm donor. "You have all of us. Plus the simple fact that you're so much stronger than you think you are. We can protect them all, babe. No one will ever fuck with our family and live to see the next day."

My hand traveled up his arm, taking in the hard, corded strength like a tree trunk. Strength he would use to protect those smaller and weaker than him.

"How do you feel about this?" I asked him. "Tell me honestly."

"Honestly?" His hand on my belly drew me closer, the other brushed my hair off my shoulder to cradle the nape of my neck. "I'm fucking overjoyed."

"Really?"

"When I was with Vicky," he paused to chuckle at my glare, "I always had this nagging doubt about her being the future mother of my kids. She was always a bit selfish and didn't respond to stress well, so I figured the bulk of the child-rearing would fall to me and I was okay with that. But you," he massaged my neck as he gazed at me adoringly, "I can't imagine anyone better. You're perfect for me, Mel, and I just know you'll be an amazing mom." He brought his lips to my ear. "And the thought of your belly growing big? Knowing my woman is carrying and nurturing my baby inside her? It gets me so fucking hard."

15

MELODY

Connor guided my hand to the front of his pants, where his hot whisper against my skin proved to be true. His lips fell to my neck, groaning as his cock filled my palm through the fabric.

"I don't know for sure if I am or not," I said, trying to not be distracted by his mouth gradually moving lower. "I haven't taken a test or anything."

"We can get one while we're here," he murmured against my collarbone. "But you know how I feel. Just tell me where you want me in the meantime."

His hand moved between my thighs, pushing them apart as he kneaded the sensitive flesh growing so hot near my core. Another groan escaped him as my fingers closed around his shaft, beginning some light, teasing strokes through his pants.

"God, Mel," he groaned, shoving me down flat on my back and pressing himself right against my core. "It feels like forever since I've had you to myself."

"I want you so bad," I gasped at the heat and pressure between my legs. "You and *only* you right now."

He hummed with pleasure as he lifted my shirt to my bra line, kissing my ribs and belly with slow deliberation. Then a pause and a smile as those gorgeous green eyes looked up at me, his fingers hooked in the edges of my shorts and panties.

"You've made me so happy, babe," he murmured, pressing more kisses to my lower belly as he peeled my clothes down my legs. "You've made me a better man. I can't wait to meet our baby, whether that's in months or years."

"Connor." I reached for him, blinking away tears. When his lips returned to mine, I didn't need to say anything else.

I needed his kiss more than I needed air. As I fumbled impatiently with his pants and took his cock, thick and pulsing in my hand, I never wanted to lose the taste of him. We only barely broke apart when I pulled his shirt off and then mine. When he aligned himself and pressed forward, filling my aching emptiness, I never wanted him to leave.

He barely exerted himself when he slid his hands underneath me to grab my ass, then lifted us both off the bed. My back met a hard wall, and he held me there, impaling me with his cock as I secured my arms around his shoulders. Our kiss never broke, and his body never left mine. We were locked, connected, and meant to be this way.

I loved the strength in his body and clawed my hands across his back and arms to let him know. Nothing about him made him lesser. He could be missing all his limbs and still be twice the average man on the street. Every person who judged him, degraded him, or turned him away, he was better than. And he was mine.

He pulled me away from the wall just as my first orgasm convulsed around him. I whimpered and shook in his arms and he just held me—one arm around my waist, the other caressing my neck as he kissed me. Strong, solid, and unyielding, he walked us across the bedroom to the vanity and gently removed my legs from around his waist.

"Turn around, babe," he said in a husky whisper, gently facing me toward the mirror. "Watch us. See what you do to me."

I watched him in our reflection, for some reason embarrassed to look at myself. His arms flexed as his hands slid down the sides of my body, then gripped his cock in his fist to enter me again. My eyes closed at the return of the sweet, delicious fullness of him, then I felt his mouth on my ear.

"Open your eyes, babe," he commanded. "Look at how fucking gorgeous you are. I want you to see yourself how I see you."

My eyelids slitted apart, catching his gaze in the mirror's reflection. His jaw tightened with restraint, his fingers dug into my hips, and every muscle in his upper body flexed so hotly as he fucked me.

Me, with my pale skin flushed rosy. With my hair fucked up and my mouth hanging open to release the sounds of my pleasure from every one of his thrusts. Me, with my hands scrambling to hold on to the vanity like I would fall off the edge of the world if I didn't. That was who he wanted, who he loved. Not only him, but two men just as incredible as him.

My eyes rolled back in my head as I came apart for the second time. But my vision returned just as Connor's whole body went rigid and his cock turned into a steel rod inside me.

"Babe, so close," he panted.

"Don't stop. Let me feel you," I pleaded, reaching back to grab his thigh.

I watched his release in the mirror. Feeling his cock flex inside me and the spreading of warmth while watching his own tremors and facial expressions nearly got me off again. I'd never seen anything hotter and couldn't get enough.

"I wasn't sure about this mirror idea," I breathed, kissing him when he leaned forward over me. "But fuck, that was hot."

"Hm, noted," he grinned, resting his head on top of my back. His rapid pulse matched mine, along with our deep, ragged breaths. "I hope our bedroom has more fun angles."

"You mean this one isn't ours?"

"Hell no. We've got the master suite." He brushed lazy kisses along my neck and back. "Gotta make room for the dragon."

We cleaned up and got dressed to return to the living room, but not before he grabbed me for one more long, lingering kiss.

"I meant what I said," he murmured. "I want a baby with you so much. But it's up to you when the right time for that is."

"Well, just now might have sped things up. If that wasn't set in motion already." I chewed my lip nervously, the weight of being pregnant now hitting me like a ton of bricks. I wouldn't be able to perform in a few months. We still didn't live anywhere permanently. Connor would stay by me no matter what, and I felt confident Raz would too, but Hunter? Things were still so up in the air with him.

I missed the hell out of him and it hadn't even been twenty-four hours yet. Did this time apart affect him like it did me? Did my absence solidify his decision at all? I was both desperate to know what choice he made and scared to death of hearing the answer. Even if he chose me, would he want a role in raising a human child?

"You're thinking too loud again," Connor teased, stroking his thumb affectionately across my cheekbone. "Don't worry, babe. Whatever happens, we'll figure it out."

"You sound like me when we first met," I scoffed.

"And you were right back then, no matter how much my negative ass tried to drag us down." He cupped the back of my neck. "Ever since you came to my trailer and ignored me when I told you to go away, everything has worked out. Hasn't it, babe?"

"It has," I chuckled at the memory. "That'll be a story to tell our kids."

"Damn right it will." He squeezed my nape and gave me one more kiss. "Now let's head back out before your dragon boy steals you from me again."

I giggled as the door opened, Connor's hands still on me as Raz and Arjun spun around from looking out at the ocean.

"Oh, for fuck's sake," Arjun whined. "Don't tell me you just shagged in my room? You've got the damn master!"

"Sorry, man." Connor draped an arm over my shoulders and unapologetically groped my breast, clearly not sorry at all. "Been a while since the lady and I had any alone time."

"Connor!" I slapped his hand while Raz smothered his laugh with a fake cough, turning away so Arjun couldn't see him smiling.

"Now I've got to call downstairs and get the sheets changed," the tiger shifter huffed, heading straight for the phone.

"If you're doing to do that, might as well have them wipe down the vanity too," Connor smirked, all too pleased with himself.

"The vanity?! Fucking hell…"

"And the wall next to the bed," I added, unable to stop myself from joining in the teasing.

"The wall too?! Fuck me, you lot are a bunch of animals."

The next sentence tumbled out of my mouth faster than I could stop myself.

"If you can't beat 'em, join 'em, Arjun!"

16

HUNTER

Normally, I could handle one day apart, or even a few. But the possibility of never seeing Mel again was too much to bear.

Seeing Colt and Gabe with Miriam made the longing for her even worse. I already knew Colt was smitten by their shaman woman, but seeing stubborn, surly Gabe warm up to her made the fierce ache in my chest cut even deeper.

The pups and I spent the day with them in their cabin, tucked back into the woods. It didn't feel right to stay in the house at the FDR Center without Connor there. They loaned it out to him after all, not me.

After spending the day in the woods and then enjoying a fresh kill for dinner with my family, I should have been content. I should have patted my full belly while looking over at my pups, safe and exhausted from living more like wolves than humans in the last few days. I should have felt grateful beyond measure that my two brothers were still alive—that my pups had more strong wolves to look up to, even if we weren't a full pack.

Before meeting Mel, I might have been content with all that.

But if I hadn't met her, I probably wouldn't be alive to see my pups content, well-fed, and happy. I might not have reunited with my brothers at all. And I certainly wouldn't be looking across the table at Colt, smiling at the human woman in his lap and missing my doe-eyed little fox with every bone in my body.

I should have gone with her. I was foolish to stay. And now I might never see her again.

When the three of them said goodnight and headed off to one bedroom, I scooped up my kids and headed for the second bedroom, grateful it was on the other side of the cabin. I didn't need their noises to rub salt in the wounds of being away from my woman.

And Razvan. I didn't realize until after kissing him goodbye how much I would miss him, too. We still hadn't established any explicit relationship between ourselves, but he was a solid fixture in our arrangement. I couldn't miss Mel without missing him as well.

I wanted more than sex with him, which I realized when he confronted me in the kitchen and I kissed him, knowing Gabe would walk in and see. I wanted Gabe to see, and I wanted Raz to know I wasn't ashamed of the connection we had. He deserved better than that.

The moment I laid my pups down and tucked the blankets around them, Rinna stirred with a whimper, then woke up crying softly.

"What's wrong, sweetie?" I pulled her close and smoothed out her hair, letting her curl up against me.

"When are we going home, Dad?" she asked between sniffles.

I hesitated, not knowing exactly how to answer. "Which home, sweetie?"

"The big house with Miss Mel, Mister Connor, and Mister Razvan," she sniffed. "And the big tiger shifter who talks funny."

My heart splintered in two. "We can go back tomorrow, honey. But Mel and the others won't be back for a little while. It'll just be us. But we can always visit your uncles."

"Why did they go away?" my daughter demanded with a trembling bottom lip. "Don't they like us anymore? Did we make them mad?"

"No, sweetie. Of course not." I kissed the top of her head and hugged her tightly. "Actually, we could have gone with them. But you had so much fun with your uncles, I thought you guys would rather stay."

"I miss Mel," she whimpered, burying her head in my chest. "I love visiting Uncle Colt and Uncle Gabe, but I want Mel back."

"Me too, honey." I blew out a long breath as I rubbed her back. "Me too."

HOURS AFTER SOOTHING Rinna back to sleep, I still couldn't doze off myself. After tossing, turning, and staring at the ceiling, wishing I had Mel's soft, feminine body and Raz's hard, tattooed one wrapped around me, I got up from bed.

Knowing sleep wouldn't come, I crept out the back

door as silently as I could. I didn't feel up for a run, but certainly couldn't lie still. I just needed something to keep my mind off the two aching holes in my heart.

"Come to howl at the moon?"

I turned to see Gabe, shirtless and leaning against the wall with a cigar in his hand. Even in the dim light, I could see the scratches down his chest. That and his smug, satisfied expression told me all I needed to know about his evening went.

"Sure, you could say that."

He handed me the cigar, and I accepted it without question, taking a few short puffs before handing it back.

"What's eating your tail, brother?" he asked. The smoke pouring lazily out of his mouth and nostrils reminded me of Razvan.

"I miss her," I confessed, leaning against the wall next to him. "I should've gone with them."

"Yeah, you probably should've," he agreed.

I looked at him in surprise. "You've really changed your tune toward humans since we met up again. What gives?"

He lifted one shoulder in a lazy shrug. "The human woman who was riding me a few minutes ago, I suppose."

"How did you two meet her?" I asked, eager for a distraction from my own love life.

"After you got captured, the pack got separated," he began. "They were trying to round up as many of us as they could, so we split up. Colt and I got chased to the edge of our territory to a small town. They set out traps and tracked us for weeks. It was safer for us to stay close to humans in the town. Our tracks were covered and we could stay together."

He took a hard pull on the cigar. "But we were forced

to scavenge since we couldn't go in the woods to hunt. We came out at night and dug through garbage cans like fucking raccoons. One night, she saw us." His lips turned up at the memory. "She worked in a grocery store and was throwing out cuts of meat. For an entire week, we waited for her at the end of every shift and she saved the best cuts for us. Finally, she came up to us and said, 'I know you guys are shifters'."

"Huh. How did that go?" I accepted the cigar from him again.

"I wanted to bolt," he admitted. "You know how it was growing up. If a human knows what you are, they might as well be putting a gun to your head. That's what Dad always said. But Colt wanted to trust her. I almost took off without him, but no way could I live with the fact that I possibly left my brother to die at the hands of a human."

"And now you're sharing her," I concluded.

"Yeah," he breathed with a small shake of his head. "It's a tough pill to swallow, you know?"

"What, sharing a mate?" I asked. "It's not unheard of among us."

"Not that," he replied. "The fact that we *need* humans on our side. Strong packs with good alphas aren't enough to keep our pups safe anymore. We have to turn to the same species, rounding us up like cattle and profiting off our abilities. I still can't fully wrap my head around it."

"Shamans aren't the same," I said. "They smell different. I'm sure you've noticed."

"Yeah," the smirk returned. "And they magic their way into our big bad hearts."

"There used to be more of them, from what I understand," I said. "So it's not a new thing to be involved with shamans, but not as many shifters know they're around."

"Miriam told us something else that makes me worry," he glanced at me hesitantly.

"Yeah, what?"

"Not all shamans can be trusted."

17

MELODY

"**B**arring any highly negative feedback from attendees, I fully expect the investment board to approve a long-term contract for you in the near future."

"That's... wow," I breathed, trying not to move my mouth too much and risk frustrating the makeup artist.

Angela Dyer sat across from me in my dressing room, tapping out messages on her phone and scribbling notes on a memo pad. All business as usual.

In the meantime, I could scarcely believe I had a dressing room at all. After crashing for the night in our suite, the guys and I showed up the next day at the time we were told, only to be ushered into separate dressing rooms. A girl offered me wine and tiny sandwiches the moment I sat in the makeup chair. I declined the alcohol but helped myself to the snacks offered.

"We've completely sold out and still have attendees scrambling to get in," Angela went on as she scrolled through her phone. I swore I heard a hint of delight in her voice. "People are posting on our Facebook page saying they're big fans of yours. Some are coming all the way from Mississippi to see you."

"Seriously?" I completely forgot about keeping my face blank. "People from Crying Falls are coming to see us?"

"It appears that way. Seems you made quite an impression in your previous work."

I sat back in the chair, utterly flabbergasted. Some attendees came to every single show back in Crying Falls, but after Connor's accident, I figured that fanbase had been too disappointed and washed their hands of us.

"I had no idea people would follow us from that far," I whispered in disbelief.

"You need your own social media pages," Angela declared, scribbling on her memo pad. "So your fans can continue to follow you. We can hire someone to manage the accounts for you."

"Oh, okay." I didn't even know that was a thing. I wished Connor was in here, pretending to be my agent or whatever again. He knew this business stuff way better than I did.

"Um, how soon after tonight would you want a new contract signed?" I asked. That had to be important information, right? I mainly just wanted to know if I'd be able to go back to Hunter and the pups again.

Angela tapped her pen on her memo pad as she thought. "It'll be a few weeks to a month before the board drafts an offer for you. Then I'm sure you'd want to negotiate the terms with your attorney, so that will add on a bit of time."

"Ah, right. Of course," I nodded like I knew what she was talking about.

"Once the contract is signed, we'd love to schedule weekly shows in time for the Christmas season. So with all the planning and negotiation involved, it'll be another few months before you're onstage with us again."

"I see." That would allow plenty of time to see Hunter again. And depending on how much money we made from this one night, I could get my siblings out of that hellhole in time for Christmas, too.

But if I was pregnant and started showing in a few months?

"How long does a contract typically last?" I asked.

"Six months to a year," she replied. "After the first run, we can arrange a traveling show if that interests you. We have plans to open more Vaudeville theaters in Texas, the Carolinas, D.C. We'd even love to have a spot right in Times Square in New York."

"Sounds great!" I forced a tight smile. "I'll have to talk it over with the guys, but I'm sure we can figure something out."

"The board is absolutely willing to be flexible with your schedule and other commitments," Angela said, leaning forward and looking over her glasses at me. "You're reliable, you put on an entertaining show, and you already have an established fan base. I'd say you're one of the wisest investments we've made in years."

Was that a compliment? It kind of sounded like a compliment.

"Thank you," I responded, keeping my smile up.

"I'll leave you to get ready," she said, rising from her seat. "If you need anything, don't hesitate to buzz me."

Not a minute after she left, a knock came to my dressing room door.

"Come in," I called nervously.

All my nerves melted away when Connor, Raz, and Arjun walked through the door. Even my dutiful makeup artist had to stop and stare at the three gorgeous men who walked right up to me.

"Man, am I glad to see you guys," I breathed.

"You clean up quite nicely, ringmistress," Arjun observed, his ocean-colored eyes taking me in from head to toe.

To fit in with the Vaudeville's corporate, polished image, they put me in a simple black leotard and jacket. For stage makeup, my look was fairly subdued, with just purple-magenta eyeshadow and lipstick to stand out against the black clothing.

"Thanks," I said, hoping my foundation and contouring covered up my blush. "Too bad I can't say the same about you."

"Oooh, burn," Connor muttered under his breath, while Raz just chuckled.

The two of them were dressed up to entertain, with Connor in a form-fitting tank top and baggy jeans, and Raz in his biker getup with a leather vest and pants, and motorcycle boots. Arjun, on the other hand, was still in the borrowed clothes that he came to Florida in. He wouldn't be gracing the stage in human form.

"Ouch," Arjun brought a hand to his chest, but his smirk told me he wasn't really offended. "I'll be happy to remain in my birthday suit, seeing as that's how you prefer me."

I gritted my teeth and dug my fingers into the handles of the chair. Ever since I blurted out the suggestion that he join us, he never stopped teasing me about it. I said it without thinking and it was a total accident. Now I couldn't stop mentally kicking myself.

The makeup artist held back a snicker as she dusted my face with setting powder. I suddenly felt annoyed that she was partial to this moment between me and my guys.

"Can you give us a minute if you're done?" I asked.

"Yeah, totally," she answered, but looked disappointed as she gathered up her brushes and left the dressing room.

"Angela said there's a pretty good chance of us getting a long-term contract," I told the guys as soon as we were alone. "People who saw us in Crying Falls have been dying to get into this show."

"That's great, steluţa," Raz beamed, the pride clear in his voice. "You entrance people. We've seen this all along."

"Yeah, but," I shifted my gaze to Connor. "That thing we talked about earlier might not bode well for any long-term deals."

"What thing?" Raz and Arjun looked between me and Connor.

Connor met my eyes calmly as he leaned against the vanity. "I can say it or you can if you want, babe. But since you've brought it up, we might as well tell them."

"Tell us what?"

I closed my eyes and took a deep breath, remembering that everything had worked out since these men came into my life. "I might be pregnant."

"Pregnant?!" Raz gasped.

"Might be?" Arjun lifted a skeptical eyebrow.

"I haven't taken a test yet but we," I nodded to Connor, "might have forgotten to use protection the last couple times."

"Ah, ah, the last one wasn't being forgetful," Connor

teased me with a smile. "I distinctly remember you telling me not to stop."

"I've heard enough already." Arjun covered his ears with his hands and turned around.

"So you were all but, ah, planning this?" Raz asked. I couldn't read his expression.

"No," I protested. "Not the first time, but I only told Connor yesterday because I was scared and we'd been so busy. We had our alone time, and he assured me everything would be okay, so it... kind of happened again." I reached for Raz's hands and pulled him close. "Are you upset?"

"I'm not upset," he muttered, stroking his thumbs across my palms. "I just would have liked to have known. Been included in that decision, maybe." His eyes flicked up to mine. "Because it affects me too, you know."

"I'm sorry, dragon," my hands wound around the back of his neck. "We should have told you right away."

"It's my bad too, Raz," Connor clapped him on the shoulder. "Since it would be biologically mine, I didn't think of you or Hunter right away. I just got so caught up in the idea of making a baby with the woman I love. Sorry, dude. We're still finding our way around this being in a harem thing."

"It's alright. I get it," Raz grunted.

I slid off my chair and kissed him hard, pouring every ounce of my love for him into it and not giving a fuck that I ruined my lipstick. "I love you, Raz, and I'd love to have your dragon babies too if I could."

That finally got a smile out of him as his arms slid around my waist. "Any baby you have, I'll love as my own. Just tell me if you're trying. Or you know, not preventing it from happening."

"I will. I promise." I kissed him again. "I brought it up because if I am, I'll have a serious bump in a few months, and they probably don't want a pregnant ringmistress onstage."

"Scheduling can get moved around," Connor said casually. "Things happen, girls get knocked up, everyone's used to it. If they're serious about us, they'll give us time. If not, we'll be in demand enough to go somewhere else that will accommodate us."

"This is why I love you guys," I sighed, staring at him while I leaned my head on Raz's bare chest. "You make me feel better and talk so much common sense when all I do is worry."

"Is that the only reason?" Raz teased, kissing my forehead.

I lifted my gaze up to him. "You support me, believe in me, and take care of me in ways I didn't know was possible. I would really be lost if I didn't have you, and I mean that."

"Love you, *steluţa*," he growled with a possessive kiss and stepped out of my reach all too soon.

"Where are you going?" I whined from my chair as they all headed toward the dressing room door.

"Almost showtime, babe." Connor winked as he followed the shifters. "And you need your lipstick fixed."

18

MELODY

Several small acts of local talent took the stage before us. All four of us would perform together last as a single act, the headlining event.

My nerves grew with every peek I took behind the curtain. The auditorium was massive, easily twice the size of the one we auditioned at in Georgia and it was absolutely packed. They filled every seat from the floor to the upper decks. I even saw security guards stop people in the lobby and turn them away.

Since the first time I ever stepped onstage, I wondered if I'd be too nervous to take that first step out into the spotlight. It was always the hardest, but now it felt nearly impossible.

We'd never put on a show like this before, combining all our talents into one cohesive performance. We only had a week, but we practiced our hearts out. Nothing should stop us from nailing it, nothing except ourselves.

When the final act finished and my drum beat started up, so did the crowd. They finished their polite applause and then got serious. Feet stomped the floor. Hands clapped together. Voices shouted our names. It still boggled my mind to hear how thousands of people could sound like a single organism. They all wanted the same thing, and that was us.

The first step is always the hardest. Do that and this show is yours, I told myself.

Feeling somewhere between fainting and vomiting, I stepped out past the curtain and my other foot followed. The spotlight bathed me in brightness, and like magic, the anxiety disappeared. Cries, cheers, and applause rang out, and a genuine stage smile grew across my face.

"Ladies and gentlemen! Boys and girls!" My voice boomed with omnipotent power through the speakers. "I see some familiar faces tonight!"

The audience only grew louder, shouting and chanting my name. Humbled, I brought a hand to my chest and smiled down at my feet.

"Thank you. I've missed you all too," I replied. "For those of you who don't me, I'm Melody, your host for this evening. Tonight, you will all meet new friends and perhaps see familiar ones, but this is unlike any show you've ever seen before. You won't believe your eyes, ladies and gentlemen! Your mind will question what is real and what is even possible. And tonight," I paused, surveying the crowd from left to right, "We dare you to believe in the unbelievable."

The stage grew dark, and I walked on my tall heels to the edge of the curtain. Low murmurs and whispers rose up in anticipation of the first act. From my place at the side, I took deep breaths, feeling just as anxious as the crowd.

When the hip hop instrumental music kicked on and the first light shone on Connor at the top of a platform, the screams and cheers hit me like a splash of cool water to the face. He didn't have stilts for this show, but he didn't need them.

He moved too fast for anyone to get a good look at his prosthetics, not that it mattered. They'd be even more in awe of him, but he insisted on not being showcased as an amputated acrobat. His routine consisted of flips and handstands like a typical acrobat, but also incorporated break-dancing and, dare I say... stripping?

Women screamed as he slowly eased down the edge of the platform to the stage floor, rolling his hips as he gripped the edges with his hands and knees. I crossed my arms as I watched, smiling with a bite to my lip as his shirt came off when he reached the floor. If I didn't know any better, I'd think this was a Magic Mike show. Everyone went nuts, and I was grateful as hell for my earplugs.

He front and back-flipped, cartwheeled, handstanded, danced across the floor, a dazzling charismatic smile on his face the whole time. My heart nearly burst for him. He actually looked like he enjoyed himself. It always seemed like he performed just because he had to. It was a job and he got it done. Now he was having fun at it, too.

The stage darkened again, concentrating a small spotlight on him, but he carried on as if oblivious. Some of the observant members of the audience noticed the small flame hovering above the platform where he began.

Connor's music faded away as the flame grew bigger, nearly the size of a person. People gasped and shouted, "Fire! Look out!"

He turned and looked up, the blaze now creating most

of the light onstage as a man's silhouetted figure stepped into the flame and drew a sword from his back. Everyone grew silent and sat on the edges of their seats as figure and flame jumped down from the platform as if they were one, and then a heated battle ensued.

The flaming swordsman swung, jabbed, and stabbed his blade at Connor, who flipped, backbended, and vaulted off the platform's vertical surfaces to dodge the attacks. Fast-tempo music accompanied the duel as Raz chased Connor around the stage.

Grabbing my prop sword from the side, I switched my mic on.

"Connor, you need a weapon against the flaming sword!" I declared. "Take this!"

Tossing it to him like we'd practiced thousands of times, he caught the handle in one hand while doing a handstand with the other. Returning to his feet, he blocked Raz's blow at just the right moment. Gasps and shrieks arose from the crowd as the human flame grew dangerously close to Connor's skin, swords crossed and pushing against each other. Even from where I stood, it looked completely real.

"I have a new plan," Razvan declared menacingly, the flames disappearing across body. His clothes and body completely unburnt, his fire concentrated along the length of his sword. Pulling the fiery blade away from Connor, he vaulted over both of us as if carried by some unseen wind and landed on his feet behind me.

Everyone screamed and shouted, "No!" when he pulled me close to his body and held the flaming sword in front of my face. I widened my eyes to show fear, watching the flames dance inches away from my face. His fire's heat was nothing more than a gentle warmth like a candle.

"Let her go, Razvan!" Connor cried out. "Your fight's with me!"

"Take her from me!" Raz cackled, walking us toward the edge and center of the stage where everyone could clearly see. "Is there anyone brave enough to free Melody? Come down and fight me if you are!"

Several men shouted back from the audience, and Raz taunted all of them.

"Ah, you've already pissed yourself in fear. I can smell it from here. You? Boy, you haven't even grown all your pubes yet. Sit back down!"

While talking shit to the crowd, Connor took the opportunity to snatch Raz's sword away. Now, with one naked blade and one on fire, he pointed both of them at us.

"You're unarmed, Razvan! No choice now but to let her go."

"Silly man," Raz sighed, lifting a hand toward his mouth. "You shouldn't play with toys unless you know how to use them." He blew across his palm, sending a stream of fire past my face and across the stage. Now both of Connor's swords were on fire.

He swung them back and forth a few times, creating a dazzling display of light which made the crowd awestruck. "I think I can handle it, you pyro."

"Come at me then!" With one hand still tight around my waist, Raz reached the other into a hidden pocket and pulled out four knives between each of his fingers. He tossed them to the other hand, juggling the knives inches away from my body. One by one, each of those blades caught fire as well.

Looking more apprehensive now, Connor approached us warily with his two flaming swords. A fight with incredible optical illusions ensued. Every jab he took looked as though it was blocked by a knife as it was tossed in the air. But Raz's juggling rhythm never broke, he just carried on. This took us nearly the whole week to get down perfectly and I couldn't be more proud and relieved that my guys were so on it.

On and on it continued, neither one of them gaining an advantage. It would have carried on forever if another small spotlight didn't appear at the top of the platform and a large feline face stepped into it.

"A tiger! Oh my god, it's a tiger!"

Raz and Connor looked up together, both of them dropping their weapons in mock surprise.

"It's Dawon!" I cried. "Here to save me!"

Arjun jumped down from the platform, eliciting gasps of shock and awe at his powerful feline form. Landing gracefully on all fours, he lowered his head and roared at me and Raz. Even though we practiced this and I knew he wouldn't harm me, the fear on my face was genuine. A tiger's bare teeth in its roaring, open mouth might as well had been looking death in the face.

"Fine, you want her?" Raz said. "Go ahead and eat her!"

He shoved me away, but the tiger remained focused on him, stalking forward to his prey. I ran dramatically behind Connor and peeked over his shoulder like any good damsel in distress.

"You don't scare me, cat," Raz told the snarling feline. "I have more skills with my blades than you have teeth!"

With that, he kicked one of his knives that he dropped to the stage floor. It hurtled toward the tiger, who batted it away like a toy. The crowd gasped, and Raz wore a look of shock on his face. He kicked up another knife and this time, Arjun caught it in his mouth. Twice more and all his knives were gone. The only thing left to do was run.

Everyone now burst into laughter and cheers as Arjun chased Raz around the stage, the dragon's knees kicking up high in an exaggerated gait, while Arjun loped around lazily just on his heels. The tension grew higher as Arjun got closer and began swiping at Raz's feet. When Raz finally got some distance, he turned around to face his pursuer and blew a massive fireball across the stage.

Laughs turned to screams as Arjun jumped right through the flames and pounced on the fire breather. Raz screamed as the massive animal knocked him to the ground. With the evil, damsel-kidnapping fire breather subdued, Connor ran up behind him for the grand finale.

He raised the two flaming swords above his head and shoved them all the way down Raz's throat.

The crowd went absolutely nuts. Even through my earplugs, I heard their cries and screams. Some were standing up in their seats and looking over as if they couldn't believe what just happened.

Raz's eyes bugged out. His hands clasped to his chest. And with a final gurgling breath, his head fell back, and he laid still. Arjun approached me and head-butted my hip, circling around me with a loud purr that radiated through the speakers. Then the stage went dark.

Just as we suspected, the audience was too shocked to clap. Without the light, you wouldn't even know the theater was packed with people. Everyone was silent, most likely holding their breath as they wondered if we actually killed a man in front of a live audience.

The four of us remained posed onstage as the lights returned. Raz was the first to move, coming to his feet with his head back and the sword handles still resting on his lips. With one hand followed by the other, he swiftly removed the now-flameless blades and held them at his sides as he gave the audience a charming smile, then took a deep bow at the waist.

The silent theater erupted into thunderous applause as the rest of us stepped next to him and took our bows as well. Even Arjun lowered his head, much to the delight of the crowd. We spent the next minute smiling, waving, bowing, and saying thank you, but crowd would not let up. Everyone was on their feet, clapping, cheering and taking photos. It felt like the applause would go on forever.

Checking to make sure his mic was off, Connor leaned over and whispered in my ear, "I think that thirty-grand just got a *lot* bigger, babe."

19

MELODY

We were rich. Or at least we would be in a few days when the Vaudeville cut us our check. For the next few hours, we signed merchandise, posed for photos, and chatted with VIP attendees. Only Arjun made himself scarce, as the theater had strict rules about animals outside of performances and we weren't about to reveal his shifter status.

Somewhere around my ten-thousandth photo with fans, a familiar pain struck the back of my head like a hammer. A vision of a woman covered in white feathers restrained under heavy shackles filled my head. In the next moment, I saw through her eyes.

"Do it, or we'll shock your kids again," said a man in a while lab coat, wielding an electric cattle prod in front of him. "Shift back until you only have feathers on your arms. Let's see our pretty angel."

"It doesn't work like that," she said through gritted teeth. "I can't just—"

Her words were cut off by the sensation of hundreds of

needles digging under her skin. I gasped in pain, clutching my side as I doubled over.

"*Steluţa!*" Raz wrapped a protective arm around me. "What's wrong?"

"I see them again," I gasped. "They're hurting kids..."

"Remember what Arjun told you," he murmured, running a soothing hand across my back. Then to someone else, "Sorry, she's not feeling well. We have to cut this short."

"Oh, okay! Can she just sign my—"

"Leave," Raz hissed. "Now."

After exerting myself in tonight's show, it took all my mental strength just to keep the pain away. The visions and sounds came through just as strong, but at least the pain was just a dull ache. Raz and Connor guided me through the backstage area with their arms around me. I could barely make sense of anything, but vaguely recognized my dressing room door being pushed open and the handsome man waiting in my chair.

"For fuck's sake! Took you all long enough playing celebrities—"

"She needs you," Connor cut him off. "The shifter visions are hitting her hard."

Through blurry vision, I saw Arjun's face close to mine. His blue-green eyes were wide with compassion as he touched my face gently. I wanted to lean into his hand, into him. He was warm, solid, and felt good...

"I can't shift here. It's too risky," I hear him say over the cries in my head. "We have to go back to the suite."

The next few minutes or hours, I couldn't tell, went by in a blur. I felt like I was drifting back and forth between two places at once. There was darkness, and then blinding bright light. I looked up at one point, realizing I was on an operating table. A man holding a sadistic-looking dental tool smiled down at me. When I screamed and tried to get up, it was Connor holding me and kissing my face.

At some point, I heard the rumbling, the sound that was so nice and comforting. I went toward it, heard it get louder, and wrap around me with warmth and safety.

I WOKE up as I often did these days—my head on a man's chest and someone else snuggled up behind me. My sigh of relief was short-lived. The suffering of those shifters was never ending. Even right now, while I didn't feel them, there were scared children huddled up in cages, their parents hurt and experimented on right in front of them.

I nuzzled my head over my man-chest pillow as I rubbed my eyes, slowly returning to the waking world. A familiar tattooed arm wrapped snugly around my waist, and I looked behind me to see Raz, fast asleep and looking adorable.

With a smile on my lips, I turned to face him. Not ready to face the world yet, I sank into his warmth. Wrapping my arms around his sides, I kissed the tattoos on his throat and collarbone until he gently stirred.

"Mm, I love waking up with you," he muttered groggily. "How are you, *steluţa?*"

"Better for now," I whispered. "But I feel awful for being here while all that is going on."

"We'll find them," he answered, pulling me in closer. "Now that the show's over, we can focus on that."

"Four of us against an entire compound? I'm simply dying to hear that plan of attack."

I froze upon hearing not only the voice, but the accent behind me. No fucking way! Was I just...

Almost too afraid to find out, I looked slowly over my shoulder. And my heart went into overdrive when my eyes confirmed my fear. I had been sleeping on Arjun's chest.

"Morning, dove," he greeted me lightheartedly, muscles flexing as he pushed himself up to sitting. "You know I don't care about this sharing business, but I must admit you are a good cuddle."

My eyes nearly bugging out of my head, I looked panicking between him and Raz. "Why... what?"

"Relax, *steluța*," Raz chuckled, kissing my cheek. "You were drifting in and out of visions in your sleep. Arj kept you grounded with his purring but seems he shifted to human at some point."

"Sometimes I go to sleep as a tiger and wake up as a human. Does that ever happen to you, Raz?" Arjun got up from bed and I buried my face in Raz's chest, but it was too late. I already saw *dat ass*.

"I've never slept in dragon form," Raz answered casually. "Not intentionally, anyway. Too risky being seen."

"I miss your dragon form," I murmured, nuzzling his neck. "Feels like forever since I've seen him."

"Yeah, it sucks not being able to shift often," he replied, then swatted my ass playfully. "But you're a shaman. You can see him any time you want to."

Hesitantly, I looked over my shoulder at Arjun. He put on pants, thankfully, but it was all I could do not to stare at his torso, which was carved better than the marble columns in the suite.

"If I do, will I be vulnerable to feeling all the other shifters again?"

"I don't think so, as long as you keep your mental shields up." He turned to leave the room, but hesitated and added, "They're getting stronger. Your mental blocks, I mean. You're doing good, Mel."

"He likes you," Raz teased once he left the room, planting kisses on my neck.

"He does not," I retorted.

"Lies," he chuckled. "Do you like him?"

I remained silent, unsure how to answer. I didn't dislike Arjun anymore. If it weren't for him, I'd probably be brain-dead or in a coma by now. And I appreciated that as a friend. He was nice to look at and listen to, but that didn't mean I *liked* him.

"I knew it," Raz chuckled at my silence.

"He's been a good friend," I relented, but he wasn't getting any more out of me than that.

"Sure," he grunted, moving his kisses down to my shoulder.

"Stop distracting me!" I giggled. "Let me feel your dragon."

"Is that code for something else?" he grinned against my skin, but stilled as I mentally reached out for the animal within him.

It was effortless this time. I was shocked at how easy it was. The beast roared as he felt my presence. He missed me, too. He longed to feel me on his back as we flew under the moonlight again. Hot, smooth scales wrapped around me in a protective embrace. I felt the wind on my face from the powerful beat of his wings, and smelled his smoky, earthy scent.

Gradually, the scales became skin, and the wings dissolved into tattooed arms that wrapped around me. But my dragon was still here. He was always here.

"I'll never get tired of that," I smiled up at Raz. "You're simply amazing."

"You are, my love," he sighed contentedly, sinking into the mattress next to me. "I'll take you to Romania one day. With all our riches, we can rent a castle out in the black forest where no one will bother us. I can let my dragon out anytime I want and fly you to the moon every night."

"Sounds romantic," I murmured, my lips against his.

"I have my moments," he chuckled, kissing me.

"One day," I sighed. "When no shifters are mistreated anymore." It felt so wrong to be here, in a luxurious suite, wrapped up in my man's arms while this compound existed. I couldn't ignore it, no more than I could ignore seeing Roo, Rinna, and Hunter that first time.

God, I missed them.

"Well, we're not getting anything done staying in bed." He kissed me once more and moved to get up.

I admired the sight of his inked physique for a moment before getting up myself. Thankfully, I was in a camisole and underwear. I'd probably die of embarrassment if I cuddled with Arjun naked.

"You say that like you know where to go," I remarked, finding a pair of shorts and pulling them on.

"I don't," he admitted, pulling on his own clothing. "But the beach is a good place to start."

"The beach?" I repeated.

"Have you been able to follow the presence of the shifters?" he asked. "Like you did when we found Arjun?"

I hadn't realized it but shook my head, frustrated. "No,

I can't pinpoint a direction for them. The visions got worse as we got closer to Miami, but I have no way of locating them."

"Arjun mentioned that last night," he said. "He's afraid another powerful shaman is working at the compound. Someone who can block you from finding it, while also projecting those visions into your head."

I couldn't believe what he was saying. "Another shaman? Letting shifters be treated like that?"

"It's possible he or she is a prisoner as well," he said. "They might be forced to do this. But if that's true, we've got another issue on our hands."

I stared at him, the realization hitting me as we said the same thing out loud.

"They already know we're here."

20

MELODY

"We just put on a show for thousands of people," I realized with increasing horror. "We were probably on the news. We'll be in newspapers and magazines. All over social media. If these are the same people who held you and Arjun, they'll definitely recognized you."

"All the more reason for us to go to the beach," Raz replied calmly. "It's public, it's crowded, we'll blend in. We'll be able to scope things out. Maybe we'll even find shifters blending in with the humans who can give us information."

I nodded. It made sense. "I don't have a bathing suit, though."

A wily grin spread across his face. "I might have gotten someone from the hotel to do a shopping errand for us."

"What?" I demanded. Then, "Wait, you can do that?"

"Dunno, but I did," he shrugged, his smile growing wider. "Do you want to see what they picked out?"

"I guess so," I shrugged back, my own smile growing

despite myself. "Over thirty-grand per show, hotel staff going shopping for us. This is my life now."

We went out into the living room to find Arjun and Connor inspecting dozens of bikinis. Every style, cut, and color imaginable laid out on the coffee table and surrounding couches.

"Jesus, how many did you make them get?" I demanded.

"Might have bought out the whole store," Raz coughed into his hand.

"Not those, babe." Connor wagged a finger at me as I went to look at a pile of swimsuits in an armchair. "Those have been rejected. These are the ones you have to choose from." He waved his hands over a smaller pile on the coffee table.

"What? But these are cute!" I picked up one with a navy blue and red paisley pattern that would cover up my chest but show off my shoulders nicely.

"Not slutty enough," Arjun quipped, nodding his head toward Connor. "His words, not mine."

"Connor, what—"

"We need to blend in to the Miami crowd, right? So you've got to wear Miami bathing suits." He picked up a stringy scrap of clothing with one finger. "Try this on, babe."

"Is that... a thong?" I looked at him in disbelief. "Connor, my entire ass will be hanging out!"

"It's what every woman in Miami is wearing to the beach." He coughed. "Not that I've been looking."

"No freaking way! I mean, wearing a bikini at all is a compromise enough. I'm not going out in a crowd of people basically naked."

"*Steluța*, you wear those stockings and corsets and shit onstage. A bikini isn't that much different."

"It's completely different!" I whipped around to face Raz, who was trying too hard to look innocent. "You didn't even want me doing burlesque onstage back in Georgia! But you're okay with this?"

"The lads do have a point," Arjun remarked. "Every woman at the beach will be wearing nearly nothing. Covering yourself up won't do you any favors if we're trying to blend in."

"Jesus, not you too," I turned on him with a glare. "You're supposed to be the brilliant one! How do I blend in without my ass and boobs hanging out everywhere?"

"Sometimes the most genius plans are the simplest, dove."

"Traitors, all of you," I muttered with a pout. "Have you ever thought maybe I don't want my body out on public display?"

"We'll all be right there with you, babe," Connor assured. "No one will look twice at you and get away with it. If someone tries to touch or catcall you? We'll knock motherfuckers out. I'm not kidding."

"Because that definitely won't draw attention," I retorted.

"Where's the free-spirited girl who jumped naked into the pool?" Raz came up behind me, gliding his hand along my lower back.

"Only you guys saw me, plus it was at night!"

"Minor little details." Raz pressed a kiss to my cheek. "We won't force you to do anything, *steluța*. But I have a feeling part of you secretly wants to show off."

"And what the hell makes you think that?"

"The lady doth protest too much," Arjun smirked.

"You like to take risks," Raz whispered seductively into my ear. "You like a little bit of danger. And you love being surrounded by your strong, handsome men."

"Don't flatter yourself," I muttered, now being argumentative just for the sake of it and they knew it. Raz kissed the spot between my neck and shoulder and my back arched in response, eliciting a pleased chuckle from him.

Damn him. Damn them all. At what point did they start to know me better than I knew myself?

"I'll try on the ones that *I* like," I relented. "But none of you get to say if it's showing off enough or not. That's for me to decide."

I got no argument from them as I pawed through the sets of tops and bottoms in search of one that, hopefully, wouldn't be downright humiliating.

A half-hour later, I left the suite wearing a little burgundy number that thankfully covered most of my ass, even though it tied at the sides of my hips in thin strings. Who said I wasn't willing to compromise? The top was a classic bikini style with triangular bra cups and strings that tied at the bra line and around my neck. My chest felt a bit more exposed than I was comfortable with, but there wasn't much I could do about that.

The guys filed close around me like bodyguards in the elevator, with Connor and Raz on either side of me, and Arjun behind us.

"Where's your swimwear, now?" I asked my Marine with a quizzical eyebrow.

"I ain't gettin' near that water," he replied. "Don't want

anything to rust. Honestly, getting near sand is probably a bit dicey for me."

He wore baggy jeans covering his legs and sneakers over his prosthetic feet. On top he wore a breezy, tropical shirt completely unbuttoned, showing off his washboard stomach and pecs that could crush walnuts if he tried.

"Oh, so *you* can cover up, but I can't?" I teased.

"I have a medical condition," he replied in a mocking, nasally voice. "Take it up with my doctor, missy."

I swatted his chest affectionately and stood on tiptoe to kiss him, during which he took a gratuitous handful of my ass.

"All this sun is gonna make my ink age faster," Raz grumbled on the other side of me. He wore nothing but blue swim trunks and flip-flops, a large beach towel draped over his shoulder. I pulled away from Connor and nestled against my dragon's side.

"I'm sure we can find some sunscreen to rub all over you," I purred, tracing my fingers across the images and lettering across his abs. It felt like a while since I really poured over the art on his body.

"God, I hope so," he grinned, draping his arm over my shoulders. "You'll need some too, *steluța*. You'll look like a lobster if you're not careful."

"Am I the only one actually looking forward to the beach?" Arjun voiced from behind us. He too was only in swim trunks and sandals, which made me grateful I couldn't see him. "The water down here is perfect. It's clean, warm enough to jump into, but cool enough to be refreshing. We can see fish, coral reefs, maybe even some dolphins."

"I don't mind the beach part," I answered. "It's the

crowds of people I'm not looking forward to."

"You got nothing to worry about, babe," Connor said gruffly, stepping closer to me as the elevator doors opened to the lobby. He placed a hand on the small of my back as we stepped out. With how close all of them, even Arjun, walked with me, it felt like nothing short of a security detail.

After obtaining a few sample-sized bottles of sunscreen at the front desk, we headed out in the direction of the ocean. It really was a breathtaking view, despite the throng of people, towels, and umbrellas dotting the white sand.

Raz's arm slowly dropped from around my shoulders and he took a firm grip of my hand, threading his fingers through mine. Seconds later, Connor did the same with my opposite hand. I didn't notice anything as we walked until I heard Arjun's chuckle behind me.

Every woman we walked past, decked out in their neon-colored bikinis much smaller than mine, checked out my men, then their faces fell with disappointment as they noticed our hands. The few who looked past them to me shot me dirty looks.

"Ignore them." Arjun's voice, surprisingly close to my ear, made me jump. "Jealous cunts." Then, to my complete shock, I felt the warmth of his hand on the nape of my neck, followed by a soft kiss at the juncture between my neck and shoulder.

"What are you doing?" I turned to look at him, utterly dumbfounded, and my pulse skyrocketing.

"Relax, dove," he shot me an easygoing smile. "They won't stop gawping, so just giving them something to gawp at."

"Well, shit. I'd appreciate a warning next time," I

huffed.

"Sorry," he muttered, the laughter gone from his ocean-colored eyes as he gazed downward. "I didn't mean anything by it."

I opened my mouth to tell him it was okay. It just surprised me, but didn't bother me. It felt really nice, in fact. My skin still tingled with the ghost of his lips and his hand on me. But I just faced forward and kept walking. I didn't want to deal with the rush of thoughts and implications if I actually allowed something to happen between us.

We found a partially shaded spot to lay out the towels and formed a sunscreen-applying train. While Connor sunscreened my back, I rubbed the white cream into Raz's back until the black dragon running from his shoulders to his waist absorbed it. He let out a sigh as I rested my cheek on his back while running my hands around him to rub more sunscreen into his chest.

"You miss him?"

"Yeah," he grunted, rubbing the sunscreen into his legs. "More than I thought I would."

"Me too." I planted a kiss on his shoulder. "It just doesn't feel the same without him here."

"I miss those damn pups too," he laughed lightly. "Never thought I was one to get attached to kids, but all their energy and happiness is infectious."

"I know. It's probably good they're not here, though. Especially if this compound is as big and dangerous as it seems."

"Yeah," he agreed. "The more I think about it, the more I can't be pissed at him for not coming. We're more or less a shifter rescue squad now and got to keep our own asses safe. It's just too unsafe for kids, especially if you're a single parent."

"You've been pretty quiet about the whole Hunter situation," I said to Connor, turning around to face him. "What do you think?"

He shrugged, peeling his shirt off so I could sunscreen his shoulders. "Neither choice is clear or easy. But he's trying to make the best choice for his kids and not himself, which is commendable. He's a great dad and a selfless person, and I'll always call him a friend whether or not he's with us. My first priority is your happiness, babe, but his will always be the pups. I can never fault him for that."

Connor's eyes flicked over my shoulder to Raz, who scooted up behind me so his chest pressed to my back and I sat between his legs. Always had to be spooning me, that one. And I loved it.

"Our check will clear in the next few days, and we'll hear about future jobs soon after that," Connor said. "The real question is, how will Razvan survive living in America's swampy asshole?"

"Heh. For thirty-grand per show, I suppose I can get used to it," Raz scoffed.

"It won't be that much at every show," Connor answered. "We can expect that much for special opening nights, but a typical show will net us somewhere between ten and fifteen if we stay with this company."

"How do you know all that?" I asked.

"I've been researching," he shot me a knowing grin. "Planning ahead, you know. For our future." Our eyes fell to my belly at the same and a nervous flutter went through me. I hadn't missed a period yet. It was probably too soon, but I was dying to know.

Raz just grunted after Connor finished rattling off numbers. "Ten, fifteen, whatever. We won't be broke anymore. It's not having those damn wolves around that bothers me more."

I leaned back against him and kissed his jaw in sympathy. He squeezed around my waist, the look in his gray eyes somewhere far off and distracted. My chest ached for him, knowing better than anyone what he was going through. He was falling for Hunter.

"Bro, you want any of this?" Connor held up a sunscreen bottle to Arjun, who remained standing and silent while the three of us lotioned up on the towels.

"Nah, I don't burn," the tiger shifter muttered. "I'm going for a swim." He started off toward the water on those long legs without another word, earning plenty of looks from bikini-clad women along the way.

"Someone's a grumpy pants all of a sudden," Connor muttered, rubbing the last of the sunscreen into his arms.

"And why do you think that is?" I asked in my best talk show host voice, only half-joking. But really, I was dying to know his perceptive insight into Arjun's behavior.

"He likes you. He touched you and you told him off. Now he feels bad for misreading things and also rejected because you told him off. So he's off to get some space and clear his head."

"Shit. You're good, Con," Raz breathed.

"And I'm never wrong," Connor added with a wink.

"Damn it," I groaned. "I really hope this one time you're wrong."

"Why?" The inquiry came from Connor. "I saw this coming a mile away. I think you did too, Raz."

"Knowing him and knowing you, *steluța*, I figured it

was only a matter of time before you two would be into each other."

"Ugh, everyone knew it but me, apparently."

"Babe, you can take four lovers or four hundred. I don't care, as long as you're happy and every one of these knuckleheads treats you well."

"Same here," Raz murmured against the shell of my ear. "As long as you still have a place for me."

"Neither of you are replaceable to me." I looked between both of them. "Not ever."

"We know."

Connor grabbed my ankles and stretched my legs out across his lap. With him at my feet and Raz at my back, it reminded me of our time in the theater room before Hunter joined in. Before my dragon and my wolf gave in to their feelings for each other.

Oh, Hunter.

My heart wasn't ready to let him go. I refused to. He was just as much my mate as the two men sitting with me now. Connor and Raz had no issue with me being with Arjun, but how would my wolf feel? If we settled here, would he really be so opposed to moving himself and the kids here?

Or was he already moving on? Building a new life without me or Raz in it?

The thought stung as I wondered what he was doing right then. Had he found a new pack with his brothers? Was he meeting females to replace the mother of his pups?

Just sitting there, stewing in those thoughts, made me so uncomfortable. I had to move. I needed a distraction.

"Think I'm gonna swim for a bit too," I muttered, rising to my feet and heading toward the water.

MELODY

I was able to find a somewhat secluded spot near some rocks at the water's edge. Some rocks made shallow pools that filled and emptied as the waves came in. I spotted a few couples making out in these pools and steered clear of them, looking for a private one to call my own.

Finally, *jackpot!* A near-perfectly round pool deep enough to sit in, with the surrounding rocks creating a barrier of privacy. I sank in and closed my eyes at the perfect temperature water washing over me. The sand and dry rocks had been nearly too hot.

I barely soaked for more than a few moments when I felt the presence of a shifter nearby. It came to me so quickly my feet kicked out in surprise, splashing like I'd nearly fallen asleep. But it was unmistakable, the first one I felt here at the beach. And even more surprisingly, this one wasn't under distress.

I reached out to feel it even more, and was surprised by what this shifter projected. Happiness, playfulness. A sense of joy, fun, and family. I felt warm sun on my skin and tasted salty water. The smile it brought to my face was infectious.

Hello? I attempted.

Oh, hello! A surprised, feminine voice answered. *Who are you?*

My name is Melody. I'm a human shaman.

A shaman? Well, isn't that interesting!

I stood from my pool and looked out over the rocks. Turning in a slow circle, I searched for the source of the voice. My senses tugged me in the direction of the water, the open ocean.

Looking for me, are you? the voice asked playfully.

Yes, I admitted. You don't have to show yourself if you don't want to. I know shifters are—

Here I am!

Out of nowhere, a dolphin broke the surface. Her tail fin slapped the water, splashing playfully as she let out a squeal before diving back underwater. A memory suddenly resurfaced of a dream I had. I saw through the eyes of some marine mammal, even used echolocation to communicate and find food.

Wow, that was amazing! I projected to her.

Aww, thank you! Sorry, I can't do it too much or more humans will come around to take pictures of me.

That's okay. Do you mind telling me your name?

I'm Waverly! Nice to meet you, Melody, the shaman.

It's nice to meet you, too, I replied. Have you talked to other shamans before?

Not for a long time, since I was a calf.

I picked up a sense of apprehension immediately after she said that.

My pod told me not to talk to any humans after that, but it's boring only talking to other dolphins!

I'm sure they're just trying to protect you, I told her. *Not all humans are good. And don't worry, I won't tell any other dolphins that we've talked.*

Pinky swear?

A slender hand emerged out of the water with all the fingers closed but the pinky sticking up. I reached down to it and saw a smiling teenage girl's face below the surface. Strawberry blonde hair spread around her head like a halo, drifting delicately in the water. Light brown freckles dotted over a petite nose and emerald green eyes looked back at me. She reminded me of my sister Jeanie, once so bright and full of laughter.

I curled my pinky around Waverly's until her hand dipped below the surface again and the smile of a young bottlenose dolphin grinned up at me.

Can you tell me about the other shaman you met? I asked her. There's not many of us around anymore.

Hmm, I don't remember him super well, but he was so nice! He brought me treats all the time like cupcakes! I never had a cupcake before and they were sooo good! I was so sad when my pod told me not to talk to him anymore.

Why did they say that? Just because he was human?

I think so, Waverly nodded her head back and forth. I heard the adults say he caught another pod with nets, but he would never do that! He was so nice to me!

Oh, wow. That's serious. My pulse picked up. Could this other shaman be affiliated with the compound capturing shifters? It sounded like he was trying to lure Waverly into trusting him when she was young. And from the sound of it, it worked.

I know! And it's not fair, she cried.

Did he tell you anything about himself? His name or his job?

He told me his name, but I can't remember. It was a weird word. She swam just under the surface in a lazy figure-eight pattern as she thought some more. *He told me he was very powerful. He trained other shamans to use their powers.*

I wish I had someone like that, I told her. *I have some help, but I've mostly learned everything myself.*

Oh, he told me had a school for shifter children! Waverly recalled excitedly. *But he said to keep it a secret because shifter parents don't like their kids being taught by humans. We're too proud, he said.*

Oh, don't worry. I'll keep that secret too, I told her, my heart now pounding wildly. It was all I could do to keep my mental voice calm. *Did he tell you where the school is?*

Here in Miami, but it's hidden. Shifters and even other shamans can't sense it, she giggled. *He said it was like Hogwarts.*

Oh, wow! I wonder if you'll get a letter, I teased her. *Would a penguin deliver it to you?*

There are no penguins here! Maybe by pelicans, she laughed, then her tone turned sad. *I'm probably too old now. Anyway, I'm homeschooled by my pod. It's true they really don't like humans involved in our lives.*

A small vibration bounced off my skin, and Waverly suddenly turned and began swimming away at high speed.

Oh no, I gotta go! I'm going to be in so much trouble, but it was nice talking to you, Melody!

You too, Waverly! I responded, as her presence grew fainter. *And hey, listen to your pod! You'll understand when you're older, but they're just trying to protect you.*

I felt her response as a sassy click through the water, and then she was gone.

My mind reeling, I sat down in my pool with my back against the rocks. I didn't want to perpetuate anti-human feelings, but it sounded like her pod had good reason to be cautious. If there was a compound of captive shifters, it only made sense to groom the young ones. Everything Waverly told me about this shaman guy gave me creepy vibes.

And if he was luring shifters to be captured, he definitely wasn't a victim himself.

The thought was inconceivable to me. Someone gifted him his powers, probably trusting him to do good with them and protect shifters from harm. And instead, he lured children to a fake school with cupcakes.

"Hey, baby doll. Want some company?"

Shielding my eyes against the sun, I peered up to the source of the voice that pulled me out of my thoughts. A balding, middle-aged man with a large belly and covered in dark hair smiled toothily back down at me.

"No thanks. I'm good," I answered, but he was already lowering his spindly legs into my pool and seating himself on the edge of the rocks.

"Aw, come on, pretty little thing. We can go party on my yacht if you want. You like Cristal?" At my non-answer, he clumsily slid into my pool, making a large splash as he purposely tried rubbing up against me. "Or we can have a private party in here," he added huskily.

"Ugh, I said no already." I recoiled and moved away, grabbing for a hold on the rock wall to get out, but the pervert wrapped a hand around my arm and yanked me close.

"Don't play hard to get, bitch," he snarled with his rank

breath in my face. "How much do you charge? Five hundred? With your attitude, that's fucking generous."

"Let me go." Rage filled me like boiling water in a kettle. "Or you'll regret it." The audacity of this man made me want to turn the water red with his blood.

"Girl, you're gonna regret opening your damn mouth." His next insult was choked off with warbling gasp and a wide-eyed stare of fear.

Because I did open my mouth, pulling my black lips back to reveal the pointed canine teeth of a wolf. And a low growl of warning rumbled in my throat.

"Learn to take no for an answer," I told him. "And I might let you live."

"What the fuck is going o—"

"Say it," I snapped, my teeth now elongating past my lips to resemble a tiger. "You will never touch anyone ever again after they tell you no."

"I'm sorry," he blubbered, now scrambling to escape back up the rocky wall. "Please don't hurt me!"

"Say it or I'll cook you slowly." Glancing down at my arms, I watched the shiny black scales cover me like armor. While no actual fire burned in my lungs, I blew out a few wisps of smoke for dramatic effect.

"I will take no for an answer," he whispered meekly.

"Louder," I demanded.

"I will take no for an answer!" He began sobbing, and I knew the dragon horns on my head made him believe all his sins had come back to haunt him. "I'll never fuck another girl again after she says no! Even if I pay her! I'm so sorry, please..."

I pulled back all the illusions I threw out, looking once again like a normal girl in a bikini. "I'll know if you go back on your promise. And next time, I won't be so kind to you."

Leaving the whimpering, pathetic man curled up against the rock, I lifted myself out of the pool and nearly ran headfirst into the center of Arjun's chest.

"Well," he remarked, looking past me at the man. "My tiger felt a pull like you were in trouble, but it seems you've got things handled."

22

MELODY

"Uh, yeah." The sight of the powerful tiger shifter knocked me off my high horse and back to feeling self-conscious. I nearly crashed into that solid, sun-kissed chest, and the fleeting memory of sleeping on him flashed through my mind. I was so consumed with teaching that old pervert a lesson, I didn't even notice Arjun's presence get closer. "Guess I did."

His blue-green gaze flicked amusedly back to me. "How will you know if he sticks to his promise?"

A smile played at my lips as I walked past him, following the length of the beach and returning to the throng of humans enjoying themselves. I walked until Arjun caught up, striding next to me on those long legs to answer.

"I won't. But he doesn't know that."

"Clever girl," he chuckled.

"More importantly," I said in a low voice, "I spoke to a young dolphin shifter who told me some pretty useful information." I repeated to him what Waverly told me, feeling a pang of guilt that I betrayed her secrecy. I never did like breaking promises, but what she told me was just too important.

"A shaman luring unsuspecting shifter children," he spat bitterly. "I can't say I'm surprised. It's the oldest fucking trick in the book."

"How the hell can someone hide an entire so-called school in plain sight?" I wondered. "Who's powerful enough to do that?"

"No one," he answered. "No one person, at least. But if multiple shamans consolidated their power? Who knows what's possible."

"I didn't even know you could do that."

"I have no idea, honestly. I'm just speculating."

We continued walking along the beach in silence, each of us wrapped up in our own thoughts. To anyone looking, we might have appeared to be a couple. We didn't touch, but why else would anyone be walking along the beach together?

Arjun only looked straight ahead or down whenever I glanced at him. He seemed to have forgotten that I was there, but he walked slowly, matching my pace as our feet sank into the warm sand as if he was in no hurry to leave.

I should have looked anywhere else, but his side profile was too attractive to tear my gaze away. Long obsidian lashes framed those striking eyes. His straight nose, high cheekbones, and angular jaw were so classically handsome, it was almost unfair. His jet black hair, reflecting the sunlight, was pulled away from his face in waves like he dipped his hands in the ocean and pushed it all back with his fingers.

"I'm sorry for snapping at you earlier," I blurted out. "I

was honestly just surprised when you did that. I wasn't angry." Still, I didn't want to outright say, *I didn't mind that you kissed my neck*, for fear of making it sound like more than it was—a simple display to piss off onlooking women.

"You did nothing wrong. It was me," he muttered, still looking just ahead of his feet. "I took it too far. I realized it as soon as it happened. You don't have to worry about it happening again."

"It's really not a big deal," I told him, his admission stinging my ego more than I wanted to admit. Had Connor read him completely wrong? "I mean, we've reached a point now where there's flirting and banter between us. It's just kind of an extension of that, I guess."

"To you, maybe. But not to me." He let out a soft chuckle. "I realize multiple partners is common between shifters and shaman, but that's not something I've ever been a part of. My mum was an old-school Indian and raised me as such. Hell, I was engaged to a girl I barely knew because our families knew each other and deemed us suitable partners. So to you, a kiss may be just be messing around, but to me, it carries a lot more weight. I acted without thinking and that's not the type of person I am."

We continued on in silence for a few moments as I processed his words.

"That's not to say I've never kissed anyone. I'm not a total prude," he tacked on before I could respond. "I'm just saying I'm from a culture where arranged marriage is common, and all of that stuff tends to happen behind closed doors after everything is official. So the whole harem thing doesn't really appeal to me, even though I'm happy for the lot of you. You're all good together, which is rare."

"So what kind of life do you see for yourself?" I asked. "Married to a suitable tigress? A family with a dozen cubs?"

"No," he scoffed. "The whole arranged marriage thing is rubbish. But truthfully... I don't know. My whole life was planned out for me. Outside of minor things, I never really felt in control. My mum and grandparents ran the show, as is customary. Then they died, and I got captured. And my whole life became focused on surviving to the next day."

"And here you are," I said. "The world is your oyster now. Or your deer kill, or whatever."

"Right," he laughed dryly. "And if I said *adios* right now? Struck it out on my own to leave you and your lovers to deal with imprisoned shifters?"

"We'd be badly disadvantaged," I admitted. "We probably are already, who knows. Not to mention the visions would be killing me without your help, but it's your choice. You owe us nothing, and you're free to do whatever you want."

He said nothing for a few moments, just chewed his lip as he squinted at the horizon.

"I never did say thank you, did I?"

"For what?"

"For that view of your arse as we walked down here," he shot me a cocky grin before saying in a quiet, more serious tone, "No, for saving my life."

I lifted one shoulder in a shrug with an accompanying sigh. "So much has happened since then, I honestly don't remember."

"Well, thank you, Melody." His hand grazed against mine and our shoulders nearly touched as we walked alongside each other. "Thank you for giving me a second chance to live."

"You're welcome, Arjun." The back of my palm lingered against his before I had to pull away, before either of us would read too much into the contact. "Even if you were a dick to me at first, I never regretted it."

"Good," he chuckled. "I don't know where my life is headed anymore, but all I know is I'm not leaving you."

WE RETURNED to where the guys camped out on the beach towels—Connor avoiding the sand like it was lava, Raz avoiding the sun like a vampire. Neither of them commented on Arjun and I walking together, thankfully.

"So what do we do next?" Raz asked after I gave the rundown of what Waverly told me.

"Honestly, I'm fuckin' stumped, mate," Arjun muttered, lowering himself to lie on the towel. "Mel can't follow anyone's presence to where the compound is. There's probably loads of shaman working to disguise the place in plain sight, and they're recruiting kids right out from under their parents' noses."

"Not to mention this has gotten shifter parents really protective over their kids interacting with humans," I added. "I'm sure Waverly's pod isn't the only family unit that homeschools them and outright forbids any contact with humans because someone they knew went missing."

"That rules out just talking to any shifter adults we come across," Raz sighed.

"Maybe not. You guys are shifters." I looked between him and Arjun. "Would they trust you more based on that?"

"Of different species? Not likely," Raz answered. "Plus,

just look at me, *steluţa*." He gestured to his tattooed body and I could see his point. My bad, sexy dragon was probably not the most approachable when it came to talking with strangers.

"When am I not looking at you?" I purred, rolling toward him.

His smile lit my heart up as he dropped a playful kiss to my nose. "You know what I mean, my love."

"I have an idea," Connor declared, sitting squarely in the middle of the second towel. "It's stupidly obvious but might also be risky."

"Let's hear it," I said, spinning around to face him.

He hesitated a long time, looking at me with a grave, intense expression. "You can sense the captured shifters, right? See through their eyes and all that?"

"Yeah, I just can't pinpoint where they're located."

"So you can communicate with them? Speaking mind to mind?"

"I imagine so. I just haven't tried it."

"Don't tell me you're suggesting what I think you are," Arjun said with a soft growl.

"You're the expert on this, RJ, not me. But what if Mel talked to them? If they gave us clues, anything. If they saw a building or went through a series of doors or something, we might be able to pinpoint their location."

"It's far too risky," Arjun replied with a quick shake of his head. "She had dozens, maybe even a hundred shifters in her head at once. If they all realize she's there and tried to answer her, she could sustain permanent brain damage."

"Can you filter them out or something, babe? So you can talk to one person at a time, maybe with RJ's help?"

"I don't know, maybe. Sometimes it was a bunch at

once, other times it felt like I was hopping from head to head."

"Mel, I don't recommend this at all." Arjun placed his hand on my leg, a sign that let me know he was serious. His color-shifting eyes narrowed in concern. "My stepfather was knocked unconscious for days when he tried to communicate with multiple shifters at once. Your brain physically can't handle it."

"What if I could stay focused on one person, though?" I asked him. "If your purring helped me to block out everything else, it would be just like Speaking with you or anyone."

"And if that doesn't work?"

My hand covered his on my knee. "We have to try. It's the best chance we have."

23

MELODY

The four of us went back up to the suite to make the Speaking attempt. At Arjun's reluctant instruction, Raz and Connor closed up all the windows and turned off every light source they could find. Focus would be best achieved with darkness and silence.

We pushed the coffee table out of the way and sat on the floor in the middle of the living room.

"What do we need to do?" Connor asked, sitting across from me.

"Say nothing and do nothing unless Mel appears to be in distress," Arjun said. "And if she does, physical touch will be most effective in pulling her back to her own mind. Raz, don't try to reach out to her with your dragon. More shifters in her head will just be confusing."

"Got it." Raz took a seat next to Connor.

Arjun sat behind me, still bare-chested and in his swim trunks.

"Skin-to-skin contact works best," he mumbled awkwardly. "I could shift to my tiger if you prefer, but then

I'll have to direct you via Speak, which just adds one more shifter voice to the noise in your head."

"Oh, okay." My pulse sped up nervously, though I couldn't explain why. I already woke up this morning with my head on his chest. "I get it. You can stay human."

I pulled off the T-shirt I just threw on and slowly leaned back until the warmth and gentle contact of Arjun's chest met my skin. The only barrier between us was my bikini string, and I wondered if he could feel how fast my heart was going from back there.

"Close your eyes," he instructed, his voice a gentle vibration on my spine. "Picture your mental shields, the ones that guard you and keep your mind safe."

"I see them," I answered, visualizing all four men at their positions.

"Now, release them one by one. Let them fall away slowly in layers. If you feel too much getting through, stop."

Panic filled my body, sending my heart into overdrive. The pain of those visions was still fresh and raw. Rather than lower my defenses, I wanted to fortify them. I knew letting the shifters through was the only way to help them, but it still scared the shit out of me. I nearly felt like dying the first time.

Just as I opened my mouth to tell him I couldn't do it, I felt the low, unmistakable rumble of a purr from his chest. It kept me anchored to this room with these three supportive men who would never let any harm come to me. With that vibration running through me, I found the strength to let go.

My first layer of defense fell away, and I stopped, waiting to see what filtered through. I saw and heard only ghostly shapes and faint whispers, so I carried on. The visions became clearer then but still felt like looking through a mask. My view was obstructed, but I knew the next phase would be startlingly clear.

"You're doing great," Arjun's voice echoed over the rumble of his purr. "Take your time, dove."

Almost unconsciously, I leaned further back against him, wanting to solidify the sensation of him in my body before my mind went somewhere else. The bare skin of my back seared to his torso until I felt the tickle of his coarse chest hair and the watery thud of his heart beneath his purr. I swore I could feel his hands on my hips, but I couldn't be sure.

"I'm here, dove. You're safe." Warmth tickled the side of my head. Was he speaking right against my ear? "You can come back or proceed. Whichever you want to do."

My body wanted to pull back. I wanted to explore Arjun physically, to be present in the room while he let me lean against him like this. I wanted to feel those fingers trail across my skin and find out what those lips tasted like...

"Focus, Mel. We're doing this to reach out to the shifters."

I thought I heard laughter and faraway voices, but couldn't be sure. I brought my attention back to the obstructed view of horror I allowed to filter through. Arjun's purr grew louder, and I drew on its strength to peel back another layer of defense.

"Remember, you're here, Mel. You're safe. We're all here with you. What can you see?"

"Cages all around me," I muttered. "Most are empty."

"You're doing wonderfully, dove. Can you hear or feel anything?"

"No, I just see."

"Good. Can you try to change perspectives? See through another shifter but only one at a time."

Different views before my eyes came and went like unrelated scenes from movies. Some were similar, but each one was slightly unique.

At first, it just looked like random rooms and corridors to me. But after a few moments of flipping through different shifter perspectives, I began to piece together what the whole place looked like. The only thing was, I didn't know what to look for.

"Look for light," Arjun's voice came through like an omnipotent entity. "A window or a door looking outside, maybe."

"I don't see one..."

Not a single window was to be seen in the place. It just looked like a maze of corridors and rooms that I struggled to keep straight. All light sources were from overly bright florescent lights, or dim, single lightbulbs in dingy dark rooms full of cages.

Then... *wait!*

I saw clear blue sky just for a half-second, and then familiar grimy walls. This shifter was paralyzed but conscious. I felt its fear and confusion, its inability to move. He or she had just now been captured and brought to this place, which made my heart ache with helplessness.

"I think I found one that can help us." My lips moved slowly, as if numbed. "Give me a minute."

Sinking deeper into the shifter's perspective, I realized this one had four legs and fur.

He was male and a young adult, but smaller than a wolf or tiger. The paws stretched out in front of me looked puppy-sized in comparison to Hunter's.

I waited, taking note of every detail I could through his unblinking eyes as two humans carried his cage through a set of hallways and doors. One, two, three, four doors away from the brief glimpse of the outside I saw. Then the humans tossed his cage like a sack of laundry against the wall, making a loud echoing clatter. From the corner of the shifter's eye, I saw other figures wince at the noise before huddling back into themselves in their own cages.

He was panicked, but his heart thudded slowly from the effects of the tranquilizer. Everything felt wrong. His mind was in fight-or-flight mode, but his body would not cooperate.

"I'm going to attempt contact," I reported to my guys through my physical body. Speaking with my own lips felt sluggish and laborious, each word a struggle to say. But I had seen through only this shifter for a few moments, and was eager to reach out.

Don't be alarmed. My name is Melody. I'm here to help you.

No, no, no! Get out! Not again! Get out of my head! Oh God, just please let me go!

I physically flinched, taken aback by the shifter's mental cries and whimpering. A soothing pressure rested on my chest, enhancing the vibration of Arjun's purr in my own body.

"Keep trying. He's just scared. Just be calm and patient." The tiger's voice was right next to my ear and yet so far away at the same time.

I will not hurt you, I promised the shifter. *I want to get you out. I want to help everyone get out, but you have to work with me.*

He talked in my head too! Why should I believe you?

I know you're scared, and you don't know me. But this is the only way I can try to get you out.

He didn't respond in words, but I felt the fear and racing anxiety in his brain. His instinct was to lash out and run, but he had no choice at the moment.

I'm Melody, I repeated. *What's your name?*

Julian, he replied softly.

Thank you, Julian, for trusting me.

What are you? he demanded, the panic in his mental voice returning. *How can you and him talk to me like this?*

We are both shaman, humans who are in tune and closely connected to shifters. We're supposed to protect you, and I'm so sorry he did this. It's not right and I'm going to do everything I can to fix it.

You're not shifter? he sounded surprised.

No, we're a rare class of humans. There aren't many of us, I answered. *I can see through your eyes, but I can't see you. What species are you, Julian?*

Coyote, he answered. *Nothing special.*

That's where you're wrong, Julian. You are special. I'm talking to you because I desperately need your help.

What can I do? I can't even move!

That's okay. Can you tell me where you were just before getting captured? Please be as specific as you can.

I was at La Hacienda to meet a guy for a lunch date, he muttered, shame creeping into his voice. *I waited at the bar and had two drinks before I figured he stood me up and got up to leave. But then I saw him looking straight at me near the back of the restaurant, so I went over to confront him.*

What happened next, Julian? I prompted gently when he went quiet.

He started going toward the back, and I followed him. I'm a lightweight, so I was a little tipsy and not thinking straight. Then he shoved me into a room and tazed me with this stick he had. It hurt so fucking bad.

I'm so sorry, I told him. *Can you tell me what happened next?*

He was in there with some other guys, and they kept yelling at me to shift. I didn't want to, but they kept saying they were going to kill me, so I did. Then they kept trying to inject me with something. I fought back, but I'm not big and strong like a wolf, you know. They hit me and tazed me some more until I stopped fighting. Then they injected me with the stuff, threw me in a cage and here I am.

Julian, you have been so incredibly helpful, I said. *And believe me, you are so brave and strong. Those men are monsters and I'm going to bring them down.*

I hope so. I'm starting to get some feeling back and it really hurts.

His pain became mine as I cemented my consciousness in his body. His jaw was swollen and tender, with the taste of dried blood on his tongue. Pain along his ribs made it difficult to breathe. I took in every sensation in his body and made it my own. Julian's pain was my pain, and he would not suffer any worse.

Julian, I need you to tell me a bit more if that's okay. About how far from the restaurant did they take you to this place? Did they get in a car? A highway?

No, they walked. It was definitely less than a mile. Tons of regular humans saw me. I think they were disguised as animal control or something? Their uniforms kind of looked like it.

Great, that's super useful! How about the man you were

supposed to meet? Had you gone out with him before? What did he look like?

No, it was our first Tinder date. He was clean shaven with salt and pepper hair, blue eyes, dressed nicely in a suit. His profile said he was 51. I, uh, kinda have a thing for older men.

No judgement here, Julian. I allowed a soft chuckle. *But seriously, you're amazing for recalling all of this in such vivid detail. I have to go now but—*

Wait, you're leaving? No, please don't go, Melody!

Julian. I could feel his panic rising, his heartbeat now elevating as his nervous system began to wake up from the tranquilizers. *I'm not leaving you alone. I just have to tell my mates—*

Don't leave me! Oh, please don't leave me! They're going to hurt me, I just know it!

Julian, please calm down. Be strong for me. I know you can.

His pleas turned into unintelligible whimpers, and cries as he pawed at the wires of his cage. Through his eyes, I saw other shifters began turning their attention to him. I smelled their curiosity and suspicion of this once-silent captive now causing a ruckus. As much as it broke my heart to do so, I had to leave him and return to my own body. But I couldn't help but try to soothe him with one final message.

You'll be freed, Julian. I promise you.

WHO IS THAT? WHO ARE YOU?

A SHAMAN? COULD IT BE?

HELP US! GET US OUT OF HERE!

All at once, it felt like ten people were yelling at the tops of their lungs directly next to my ear. I couldn't even feel the vibration of Arjun's purr anymore, it was so loud. A sudden, stabbing pain threatened to split my head apart, and the noise became too much, a deafening roar of too many voices. I clasped the sides of my head, which did nothing to muffle everyone out considering they were already in my head.

Hands grabbed at my arms, legs and waist, but I couldn't come back. I couldn't hear my guys over the voices in my head. All the shifters screaming and pleading for my help felt like they were sucking me into a black hole.

"Mel... Mel... please..."

Lips covered mine, smothering my breath in a kiss that tasted unfamiliar, but too good not to kiss back. A soft tongue caressed mine, followed by a hand pressing to my cheek.

"She's coming back..."

Why was I so tired? I could barely open my eyes.

The voices began to fade, but that searing, splitting pain remained, even when the world went dark.

24

MELODY

The pain never went away. Somehow, I was aware of it even while passed out. Like the antithesis of Arjun's purr, it was a constant reminder of suffering, not soothing.

My head swam as I returned to consciousness. Light felt like needles stabbing my eyelids, so I shut my eyes tightly and pressed my face into the pillow, down into comforting darkness.

"Babe?"

"Mmugh."

"She's alive, at least."

"Stop talking so loud."

"What? I'm talking at my normal volume."

"She's sensitive to noise right now. Just turn it down a notch."

"Is this better?"

"Not really," I groaned. Even though I knew the guys were whispering, it still felt like screaming directly into my ear.

No one said any more, thankfully. Someone pressed a piece of paper into my hand and I cracked open one eye to read it.

Do you feel well enough to tell us what Julian told you? -A

I couldn't help but smile through the pain. How considerate of him to ask me without using noise.

"Testing. Mic check. One, two, three." I murmured into the pillows.

Light, muffled laughter followed, and I knew the guys were trying to keep from making as much noise as possible. My own voice didn't bother me nearly as much, so I repeated everything Julian said before the other shifters somehow heard me. After a few moments, another note pressed into my palm.

Thanks. Your consciousness was so deeply entwined with Julian's that when he started to panic, you did too and lost focus. The other shifters began filtering in and that's how they heard you. -A

"Sorry," I murmured into the pillows. "He was so scared, and I was just trying to comfort him. I didn't mean to make you all worry."

I got no words back, but a soft kiss accented by the caress of a split tongue danced across my shoulder. Another kiss, this one with a normal tongue, pressed to the exposed skin of my waist. Someone moved on the bed next to me, and then stopped as if hesitant. I thought everyone had left until a hand gently caressed my palm.

"Thank you, guys," I sighed, weariness settling over me. "You're all the best. Even you, Arjun."

THE PAIN in my head faded to a dull, throbbing ache when I woke up again. The curtains had been pulled across the windows, sending the room into darkness. When I dared to push them back an inch, darkness greeted me from outside as well, with street lamps as the only illumination.

Murmured voices floated through the closed bedroom door, along with a bright strip of light peeking through the crack at the bottom. I moved toward the door slowly until my ear pressed to it, testing my sensitivity to light and noise. When the pain didn't worsen, I cracked the door open slowly, allowing the outside light to spill into the bedroom.

"There she is."

Four pairs of eyes looked at me as I blinked to allow my eyes to adjust. Wait, *four?*

I rubbed my eyes and blinked harder, then an ugly sob escaped my throat.

"Am I dreaming?" I asked no one in particular as my gaze settled on the gorgeous man with shoulder-length platinum hair and golden eyes.

"No, you're not, little fox," Hunter answered, a smile playing on his lips as he rose from the couch and strode over to me.

"What... how..."

"Shh." He pulled me into his chest when I just stood there dumbfound, stroking my hair with a soothing hand. "God I missed you, my beautiful girl."

"I missed you," I whispered, coming out of my stupor to send my hands up his long, solid back. Nothing ever felt so right.

He tilted my chin up to look at him, those eyes as deep and endless as amber. "Can you forgive me, Mel? I was so wrong, my love. My place is with you, and it always will be."

"But the pups?" I blinked up at him. "Roo and Rinna? Don't tell me you—"

"They're back home with my brothers," he assured me with a hand on my cheek. "It's just temporary. Whatever the group decides, whether settling here or going back, I'll get them when we make a decision."

"But are you sure they're okay?" I demanded. "You didn't want to leave them even for a day before. And who knows how long—"

"Colt, Gabe, and Miriam will protect them with their lives," he said, conviction in his voice. "I have no doubt of that. And Miriam has a phone, so we can video chat and check in whenever."

"What about the fact that they're your pack? Your family?" I asked, eager to squash the last nagging doubt in my mind. "They're wolves, like you. You don't feel like your place should be with them?"

"They are my family," he agreed. His hands then fell to the curve of my waist, where he pulled me flush against him with such dominance and possession that my knees turned to jello. "But *you* are my mate," he growled. "My place is at your side."

"Hunter..." His name rolled off my tongue like an erotic moan, and we weren't even naked yet. My brain just couldn't process seeing him again after fearing I never would, and craving him like he was my first meal in days.

"They filled me in on everything, little fox," he told me, his lips hovering barely an inch from mine. "The compound, a shaman kidnapping people," he paused, a smirk forming on his lips as he cupped my chin, "and I heard you may or may not be trying for a baby."

"Well, ah." His eyes, that mouth, his smell, were all too intoxicating for me to focus. His body too hot and pressing hard against me. "One thing at a time."

I stretched on my tiptoes to reach his lips. He closed the distance and lifted me up, allowing my legs to wrap around his slim hips. Our kiss was a desperate, hungry clash of teeth and tongue. I swore the lingering pain in my head floated away as his fingers dragged sensually across my scalp. His growing erection pressed against the center of my heat, sending jolts through my clit.

After feeling like I got hit by a truck, he was exactly what my body needed. Not that my other men didn't feel good, but no one else was my wolf. He was my missing piece, the reason why I felt so complete and right and just better.

In a tangle of arms, legs, and kisses, we dropped to the couch and I couldn't hold back the moan from his resulting thrust against me.

"We'll give ya some alone time," Raz chuckled to the left of me.

"No, wait." I broke the kiss and reached to grab his arm. "Stay with us, dragon."

25

HUNTER

Raz's eyes raked lustily over me, much like they did when I showed up at the door. But now our gorgeous woman was included in his field of vision.

"Are you feeling better, *steluța?*" he asked her, his voice thick with desire. "You're not in pain anymore?"

"Just the pain of not having you right now," she smiled at him wantonly, her temple resting on my forehead and her arm around my shoulders.

The dragon dropped all hesitation and leaned over, kissing her deeply right in front of my face as the other two made themselves scarce. Arjun immediately went to his room and closed the door, while Connor looked ready to leave the suite.

"Connor?" I inquired with a lifted eyebrow.

"Y'all have fun. I'm gonna throw back a couple and watch the game." He pulled on a jacket and dropped a kiss to Mel's head as he walked by.

"I might meet you down there after we're done," I said, leaning my head back against the couch.

"Sounds good, wolf man. Love you, babe."

"Love you too!" Mel called to him as he left the room, freeing Raz's mouth to crash down to mine.

I released a groan at the first hot, smoky taste of the dragon shifter. My mouth opened to him and savored his snakelike tongue caressing over mine. God damn, I didn't even realize how much I missed him. How much I craved his taste almost as much as Mel's.

As I wrapped a hand around his neck to deepen the kiss, Mel's soft plush lips made a trail of kisses down my neck. Another moan escaped and my hips rolled in an upward thrust as if they had a mind of their own.

With no pause in her kisses, Mel slid halfway off my lap to straddle one of my thighs, giving Raz ample room to move in closer. And he did just that, now kissing down the other side of my neck as he slid a hand up my thigh, moving increasingly closer to the bulge in my pants that begged to be freed.

"Fuck, I am never leaving you two again," I growled, writhing between my two lovers as they teased me.

"You better not," Raz growled, pulling away and meeting my eyes with a smoldering gaze. "And if you do, do us a favor and never come back. You can't fuck with our hearts like that."

"Never again," I repeated solemnly, holding his gaze before turning to Mel. "I promise. You're my mates. Both of you."

Raz let out a small gasp of surprise, but Mel just smiled as she kissed me sweetly, her small fingers trailing with aching slowness down my chest. The moment her mouth broke away from mine, Raz turned my head back to face him.

"You mean that?" he demanded, eyes now wide with disbelief. "Mates? You and me?"

That word carried a lot of weight in the shifter world, and I used it purposely. A mate was so much more than a hookup or a fling. It was a partner. A lover and friend wrapped up into one, often for life. A close, unique bond that was rare to find.

I thought I found that in my pups' mother, but that bond didn't hold a candle to what I felt for Mel, or this dragon shifter that knew how to light me on fire. I was the luckiest fucking wolf in the world to have two mates, and for the two of them to have each other.

"I mean it, Raz. Trust me, I thought about it on the long-ass bus ride here." I took one of his tattooed hands and placed it over my heart. "You're my mate just as much as Mel is."

The look on his face was unreadable before his mouth crashed to mine and Mel made an endearing, "Awww," sound.

"I'll show you *awww*," Raz growled against my mouth, then pulled her across my body as she squealed.

His kisses to her were as rough as mine, manhandling her as he tore off her top. He swallowed her moans and mewls as he rolled her nipples between his fingers until they were tight little buds. I followed suit with her lower half draped across my lap, dragging her shorts and pants down her long legs.

My cock turned to iron at the sight of her gorgeous, heart-shaped ass so close. Listening to the sounds of Colt and Gabe being with Miriam while my woman was hundreds of miles away was downright torturous. Now she was here in the flesh, and I couldn't stop running my hands over her delicious curves.

A moan and a soft slurping sound drew my attention up toward her head. Raz was just peeling his shirt off his tattooed arms while Mel's head moved in his lap. His jeans were unzipped and shoved haphazardly down his thighs, like she wanted his cock so badly she couldn't wait until his pants were off. He shot me a lazy smile as he stretched his arms across the back of the couch.

"Welcome back to heaven, wolf," he sighed happily.

"It's good to be back," I said, trailing a finger between Mel's thighs to gauge her wetness. "Fuck, she's soaked."

She twitched and squirmed as I rubbed her slit, her moans muffled by Raz's cock, when I circled around her clit. My own erection pressed so hard against my zipper, it was nearly painful. With one hand still playing with her, I used my free hand to work myself out of my jeans.

"Need a hand there, wolf?" Raz's eyes danced hungrily as he watched me.

A nervous thrill zipped through me. *Dare I say it?*

"A hand would be great," I told him. "But your mouth would be even better."

The pleasure lighting up his face was absolutely priceless.

With a bit of scooting and adjusting, our dragon got into position and took his time. First he kissed me, slower and more sensually than before. I sensed he was giving me room to change my mind, knowing I never had another guy do this to me before. But I kissed him back hard, shoving my tongue in his mouth and letting him know what I wanted. I said he was my mate, and I fucking meant it.

He began kissing a trail down my chest and I took the opportunity to take in his tattoos, to inspect the art I never got such a close look at before. My fingers skimmed over the black dragon covering his back, the nude woman on his arm, the knives on his ribs. When his mouth reached my navel, my fingers dragged across the flowing lines on his scalp, barely visible through the density of his dark, buzzed hair.

And when he pulled my jeans away from my hips and flicked both sides of that tongue against my cock, all I could do was press my head back against the coach and let out a wordless, animalistic moan.

His voice vibrated against my shaft as he took more of me in mouth, and only then did I remember Mel was still sucking him too. I pulled my gaze away from him to watch her, my cock swelling as his piercings slid past her lips. Letting him pop out of her mouth, she continued stroking him with her hand as she looked over her shoulder at us.

"Fuck," she breathed, her eyes glued to Raz, now taking more of me down his throat.

"You got that right," I rasped, my fists clenching as his lips easily reached my balls. Jesus, how many other guys could say they got sucked off by a hot, tattooed sword swallower?

To distract myself, I returned to playing with Mel's pussy. Her beautiful ass was still draped over my thighs, but her heat and wetness only walked me closer to the edge where Raz was taking me. Her moans and whimpers, with her face stuffed full of dragon cock, didn't help either.

She ground her hips against my hand as I rubbed her

clit. Her moans grew louder, more frantic, her thighs quivering as she neared her release. My balls felt like lead as Raz teased that tongue along my shaft, my cock bordering on painfully hard as our perfect circle of pleasure heightened, nearing its peak. When his hand squeezed around my balls, I knew it was over.

My release exploded in his mouth with a force that was nearly violent. With the way he jerked and moaned as he swallowed me, I knew he just gotten off too.

"Stop touching her for a second, wolf," he instructed once his mouth release me.

"I'm so close," she whimpered.

"I know. But I can't let Hunter have all the fun," he grinned.

He got up and sat on the other side of me, letting Mel's legs stretch out over his lap. After smoothing his hands over her ass for a moment, his finger stroked along her slit, making her shiver a few times before inserting them.

"Now you can play with her clit again," he told me.

With his fingers stroking inside her, and my firm pressure on her clit, we made our woman orgasm at least six times until she told us she physically couldn't anymore.

26

ARJUN

I turned the volume on my TV all the way up to drown out the noises from the living room. A knock pounded at my door after about an hour.

"Yeah?" I called, muting the TV.

"It's Raz. Let's go out, Arj."

I pulled open the door to see the dragon shifter surprisingly fully dressed. "Thought you had plans for the evening?"

"We ah, had a nice little reunion," he flashed a grin. "But we've got a restaurant to scope out. So why don't you and me hit the town?"

I hesitated, feeling an intense push-pull within me. On one hand, I wanted to stay curled up and hidden in my room. On the other, I was dying to get out of this suite and put as much distance as possible between myself and Mel, at least temporarily.

"Yeah, alright," I relented.

I followed him out to the living room, the smell of sex and sweat drifting in the air like a breeze. A human nose wouldn't pick it up, but it made my tiger growl and stretch his claws out. He needed a mate and was convinced she was the one. She smelled right. She was strong, kind, and a sight for sore eyes. I knew and understood the pull he felt —it was animalistic and instinctual. But it could never happen.

The woman in question stood next to the door, a rosy blush on her cheeks and a relaxed, blissed-out look in her eye as the only evidence of what just happened here.

"Hey," she greeted with a shy smile. "Sorry to, uh, make you run off to your room like that."

I shrugged as casually as I could muster. "As long as you bleach the couches and whatever other surfaces you've tainted, I'll forgive you."

She laughed, giving me a playful smack on the arm. Part of me was glad she didn't have such a big stick up her arse anymore, and was coming around to understand me. The other part wished she would still huff and throw a fit. This would be a lot easier to deal with if she still clearly detested me.

"Where are you lot off to?" I asked when Hunter emerged from the restroom and joined her by the door.

"Meeting Connor down at the bar to watch the game," Hunter answered, squeezing Mel's nape. "Maybe see about some food and video chatting with the pups."

"Yes, let's go! I'm dying to talk to them," she urged before turning to Raz. "Be careful. Both of you. Keep us updated."

"Of course, *steluţa*," he murmured, nuzzling and kissing her as the four of us left the room. He kissed Hunter as well, then we parted ways with Mel and the wolf taking the fancy, winding staircase down to the lower levels, while Raz and I heading to the elevators.

"You don't have to make this so difficult for yourself, you know," he said, looking straight ahead as our elevator doors slid shut.

"I don't know what you're bloody talking about," I sighed.

"Come on, you big pussy. Do I have to say it? You and her."

"Sorry, did you say something? Because I swear you just spouted a bunch of bollocks that doesn't exist."

The elevator ride was blissfully silent until the moment we reached the ground floor.

"So, are you going to tell her it was you kissing her that brought her back?"

With a soft ding, the door slid open, and I walked out into the lobby without answering him.

"She deserves to know," the pesky lizard continued as he followed, hot on my heels.

"And what good would that do?" I said with more snarl than I intended. "Nothing else was working to bring her back."

"That's bullshit, Arj. I know you better than anyone here, so I definitely know a kiss means more to you than most. You wouldn't have done it without a reason."

"The reason was to prevent from her brains from becoming scrambled eggs."

"Right," he huffed. "Next you're gonna tell me there was a legitimate reason for that skin-to-skin contact?"

"I could catch glimpses of her visions while touching her, so I could guide her and keep her focused. Plus, she could feel my purr better that way. Now where the fuck is this place?"

"I looked up the address. Follow me." Raz took a hard left out the hotel doors and turned to face me, pushing them open with his back. "We're not done talking about this, by the way."

Finding La Hacienda, the restaurant where Julian had been set up, was easy enough. It was at the center of Miami's night life, complete with flashing neon lights, human men wearing too much cologne, women in the tightest dresses I'd ever seen, and loud club music blasting from neighboring establishments.

I followed Raz's lead up to the bar, quietly surveying the dark corners and clientele of the place.

"Two fireball shots," Raz ordered, flashing me a smile. "Drink this and you'll get a small taste of what it's like to be a dragon."

"Ugh, I'd rather not." My stomach churned at the sickly sweet cinnamon smell that poured from the liquor bottle.

"Come on, you big prick. Just one."

"Hey, aren't you that one guy?" the bartender looked dumbfoundly at Raz, nearly spilling as he poured the shot.

"Depends who's asking," Raz answered.

"You were in that show last night! The sword swallower, fire breather guy!"

"That's me," the dragon chuckled amusedly.

"Well, shit, that was amazing! These are on me tonight! Where's the rest of your group? We'll treat them too!"

"Enjoying a quiet night at home. Just me and my boyfriend here tonight." He threw an arm around my shoulders and slapped my chest affectionately, ignoring my glare.

"Well, you boys just flag me down and I'll take care of whatever you need." The bartender winked suggestively and I only then noticed the rainbow-colored wristband on his smart watch.

"For fuck's sake, Raz," I groaned when he walked away, rubbing my forehead.

"What? Live a little! You're a free man now, no need to brood and pout." He clinked his fireball shot against mine. "Drink up. To beautiful women *and* men."

"You're in a good mood since the wolf returned," I observed, choking back the shot.

He nodded as he swallowed his drink, his face flushing red from either the alcohol or what I said. "It's a fucking rollercoaster, man. First, Mel scares us to death and we're all worried about her becoming a vegetable. Next thing we know, she's okay and our missing lover shows up." He leaned heavily against the bar with a sigh. "Can't make this shit up."

Over his shoulder, I noticed a shadow flicker across the wall. To human eyes, it looked like nothing but my tiger perked up. Alert, ready, and dying for a hunt.

"Don't make any sudden moves," I told Raz, leaning in closer and speaking in a slow voice. "But looks like someone just headed to the back room where our boy Julian got fucked up."

He gave the barest hint of a nod and drummed his fingers on the bar top. I knew he was using his reptilian senses to pick up the vibration of the man's footsteps, gauging distance, direction, and movement.

"Excuse me," I raised a hand to get the attention of the

bartender, and he came eagerly running over. "Where's your restroom?"

"Down the hall and to the left."

"Thanks." I leaned close to Raz's ear before leaving. "Meet you around back."

He grinned, chuckling to himself as if giddy with my display of propositioning him, but I knew he was genuinely amused. I could play the part if need be.

Making my way down the hall, I quickly picked up the scent of the man who headed back here a moment ago. He smelled like blood and tranquilizers, a cocktail of scents I was all too familiar with. More faintly, I picked up a mixture of scents I didn't recognize. Probably all the shifters that got dragged back here.

The hallway and scents dead-ended to an unmarked door painted black. I tried the handle, but it didn't budge. I could've broken it down, but figured that would draw too much attention at this stage. Mel did warn us to be careful.

Retracing my steps down the hall, I exited the restaurant through a side door to find Raz waiting for me in the alleyway.

"He's moving fast," he warned, taking off at a spirited, but still leisurely pace.

"It's alright, I can smell him," I replied, walking alongside him. "Julian said he was in walking distance, so we'll find it soon enough."

We walked a few blocks following our respective trails when the scent suddenly disappeared. I stopped, did a double-take, then walked a few steps back the way we came. Yes, still a strong trail there. Then a few steps forward and nothing.

"What the fuck?" Raz growled in frustration. "I can't feel shit anymore. It's like he just became a statue. Can't even feel a breath."

"Yeah, his scent stops right here." I pointed at the sidewalk, drawing an imaginary line with my finger.

"How is that fucking possible?"

"An illusion," I realized, lifting my face to the sky. "A fucking magic trick."

"Arjun," Raz stared at me. "What do you mean?"

I picked up a pebble and tossed it straight up in the air. About a foot above our heads, it hit something unseen with a metallic clang sound and shot back down to the earth.

"We're dealing with a shaman who can cast illusions not just over themselves but entire areas of space. Fuck, I should've known..."

The world spun around me and I felt violently ill. I didn't feel this sick after eating roadkill for the first time. All the signs were there. A hidden "school", a man in his fifties. Oh Shiva, how could I have been so blind. I leaned against a lamppost and tried not to lose the contents of my stomach.

"Arjun?" Raz grabbed my shoulder and attempted to shake me back to my sense. "Should've known what?"

I couldn't meet my friend's eyes to say it.

"That my stepfather, Lhozen, is behind this."

THANK you so much for reading *Tightrope!* The epic finale is ***available now in Curtain Call!***

NEWSLETTER & READER GROUP

Never miss a book release, plus get three *free* short stories when you sign up for my newsletter!

Grab your freebies at:
    crystalashbooks.com/freebies

You can also join my reader group on Facebook to get updates and hang out with fellow readers.

Join Crystal's Coven at:
    facebook.com/groups/crystalscoven

ABOUT THE AUTHOR

Crystal Ash is a USA Today Bestselling Author from California. She loves writing steamy, heart-wrenching romance with tortured heroes, especially if they're in a reverse harem. Crystal's other loves include animals, mythology, and well-crafted alcohol, most of which can also be found in her stories.

When she's not writing, she's probably drinking craft beer with her husband or trying to coax her feral cat into accepting affection.

crystalashbooks.com

facebook.com/Crystal.Ash.Romance
instagram.com/crystalashbooks
amazon.com/author/crystalash
bookbub.com/profile/crystal-ash